From the peep palaces of Times Square to the cubicles of corporate America, Sam Lipsyte's stories comprise a chorus of gallows humor and good will gone bad. There's Gary, failed punk icon turned petty drug dealer and amateur self-actualization guru, and the Chersky girl, who makes a strange midnight discovery roller-skating through a morgue. Pot-dazed Trotskyites, summer-camp sadists, and morally-ambiguous babysitters also make themselves known in the lost, shattered landscapes of Venus Drive. *In these visceral, sharp-witted tales, Lipsyte serves up a modern buffet of hope, lust, and loss.*

"It's a dark thrill to tap into the sensibility of Sam Lipsyte's remarkable stories. Not only does he write with comic-tragic brilliance, he knows something terribly important about the zeitgeist. Venus Drive is a dazzling debut." —*Robert Olen Butler*

"You know what I did when I was your age? I kept trying to be the first person on my block to be able to say I had just read so-and-so. Can you believe it? All I wanted was to hurry up and spot an emerging writer, somebody nobody else sounded anything like. Pretty nutty, you bet, but it turned out to make a life for me, which is a lot more than I can say for some of the other stunts I was pulling when I was your age. Wise up. Try out Lipsyte. Walk around with his stories. See if they look good on you. Drop the name. Say Lipsyte. The gang of them, they'll stare and say who, who? Which is where you'll already be so far ahead of the game, it won't even be funny, will it? Now tell me who ever gave you better advice. And what's it going to cost you? Please. I'm handing you a way of being, or at least a way of seeming to be, for the price of one stinking lousy one-of-a-kind book." —*Gordon Lish*

"Sam Lipsyte's stories are short and not so sweet: more like a dash of salt water in the face of life this minute, as if to say 'Wake up, friend, let's get crazy!' And the getting is excellent."

—*Barry Yourgrau*

"These are terrible people doing terrible things! There must be something redeeming about them, right? What I know is that Sam Lipsyte can write: he juices the American language into some lyrical, terrifying pulp. Drink it up if you dare. His stuff is so scary, it's good."

—*Will Blythe*

Venus Drive

Stories by Sam Lipsyte

OPEN CITY BOOKS

OPEN CITY BOOKS
225 Lafayette Street, Suite 1114
New York, NY 10012
www.opencity.org

Designed by Meghan Gerety

Cover photograph by Dolorès Marat
Author photograph by Michael Galinsky

Manufactured in the United States of America

10 9 8 7 6 5 4 3 2 1

Library of Congress Catalog Card Number: 99-068410

ISBN 1-890447-25-0

These stories have previously appeared in the following publications:
"Torquemada" in *The Quarterly*; "The Morgue Rollers" in *5_Trope*;
"Cremains" and "Old Soul" in *Open City*.

In Memory of My Mother

Contents

Old Soul

You could touch for a couple of bucks. The window of the booth went up and you stuck out the bills. They might tell you not to pinch, but I was a stroke type anyway. Some guys, I guess they want to leave a mark. Me, I just like the feel.

I went over there on the way to see my sister. There was a lit-up eye with an eyebrow over the door, a guy in front with a change belt, an apron that said Peep City. Peeptown was up the block. They didn't have an eyebrow over the eye over there.

Why do they make these places so dark? I like to cop tit in the light. Guess I have no shame. Maybe I got through shame a long time ago. Somebody said I had an old soul, which I took to mean I'm older than I am, or that I've been places I haven't been.

You could hardly see in there, in Peep City, and all that disco, that ammonia, it made me sick. I looked around for a girl with a good set, one who would maybe tell me I was sweet. Sometimes they asked about handjobs, blowjobs, all the jobs, but I never wanted to go that far. I felt sorry for them. Somebody told me they were exploited. Me, I always paid in full.

This time, just to break habit, I went for what one of them had down below, a few bucks more. She was a giant with plenty on the chest, but I put a fivespot out. She swiveled on the ledge, pushed an ass dusted with glitter out over the sill. I palmed her there, thumbed a pimple near the crack. What am I paying for this for? I thought, thumbing it.

The giant was talking to another girl pressed against her

on the ledge. The other girl was a sway of hair that moved like a metronome. The sway took on the color of the strobes.

"What's he doing down there?" said the other girl.

"Jeez, nothing," said the giant.

I dug a knuckle in.

"What the fuck," the giant said. The blind was buzzing shut.

"Prick," she said.

There was a bucket near the door with soapy water in it. I got down like you do for a shoelace, dipped my knuckle in the bucket. The man in the apron came up.

"I got ass germs on it," I said.

I figured it was Peeptown from now on.

There were still a few hours before my sister's visiting hours were over, so I went to visit a friend. This was the guy who explained to me how the girls in Peep City were exploited. The ones in Peeptown, too. He worked the graveyard in the shipping room of a superstore. Another year, he told me, and they might let him come upstairs. He worked mornings in his apartment, stuffing envelopes, selling pot. A guy like that, you hope he has a secret calling, or maybe a guitar. But Gary just wanted to live. Or maybe he thought he wanted to be free. Some do.

When I got there Gary loaded up a pipe and passed it over. I told him all about Peep City, the pimple, the girl.

"You should stay away from that place," said Gary.

"I don't have much choice now," I said.

"All those places, man. Your soul is sick."

"I thought you said I had an old soul," I said. "Now it's sick."

"It's an old sick fuck," said Gary. "Go see your sister.

You're going to be sorry you didn't see her."

"I've got time," I said.

Time stops, goes, stops again. When you have an old soul like I do, everything gets old really quick. Nothing is new. An avocado, a glass of beer, it all tastes like it's been sitting out on a table too long.

Gary fell unconscious from all his freedom. I found happy hour somewhere. I knew the bartender, a brush cut from the big one. He was German, the other side. All he had now were a few shelves of New Jersey vodka and a thing about the Jews. I let him rant. I figured with a soul as old as mine, maybe I fragged his brother at the Bulge.

"I'm an old soul," I told him.

"Oslo? Fuck it."

"Not Oslo," I said.

"No souls," he said. "Fuck it. Norway, too. Odin is a yid."

A girl in a tank top got up in my lap. She didn't smell, but her shoulders, her hair, they had a dirt sleep shine.

"You look like that rock star," she said. "Do you get high?"

"I am high," I said.

"No, I mean high."

"Oh," I said. "Sometimes."

"You're buying," she said.

We went someplace, her place, her boyfriend's, her mother's, who could tell? You can't tell from a sofa. Or a couch. You can't tell from a coffee table, or a cross on the wall. She took what we bought and locked herself in the bathroom. I was on old soul time. I lost track of bathroom time.

"Sandy?" I said. She'd know who I meant.

I was getting ready to break down the door. I was getting ready to be the guy who has to tell the whole story to the police, and maybe get punched by them for being the guy who was there on the sofa, the couch. The door opened and Sandy came out, clean and wilted in a towel. Her hair smelled of honey, or hibiscus, one of those. Her eyes were pinned and she handed me a bag, some works.

"There's bleach in there," she said.

"No, thanks," I said. "I just want to take a leak."

I stood over the bowl but I couldn't get flow. When I lie about having to take a piss, I can't piss. I stared at the wallpaper, woodpeckers. On the beaks, or on the breasts of some of them, and on the leaves of trees, was a fine red spray. It was on the rim of the bowl, the tiles, too.

I went back to what I was sitting on and sat with her.

"I guess I should blow you," she said.

"I have to go," I said.

"Don't leave."

"You can keep what we bought," I said.

"You're nice."

"I'm sweet," I put my hand in her tank top, on whatever her habit hadn't eaten off. "Aren't I sweet?"

"You're sweet," she said.

"I have an old soul," I told her.

"What do you mean?"

"I'm advanced," I said.

"I'm intermediate," she said. "I got a badge in camp."

I took a train uptown to where they were tending to my sister. There's a whole block of enormous buildings for people who are running out of luck. My sister was in the Someone-Someone Pavilion. Ventilator, feeding tube, they had everything in her to keep her from going anywhere.

There was a guy in the room I knew from somewhere. High school. Homeroom. Guess he had a name with the same first letter as mine. I once caught him with his finger in my sister under the Ping-Pong table. When he saw me that time he pulled his finger out. Don't be a schmuck, I told him, finish up. Now he had his hands on his knees, a book in his lap.

"Good thing you came," he said.

"How is she?" I asked.

Close to the bed, I saw what a dumb question it was. My sister used to be pretty for her type. She was still pretty, if you like girls who are skulls with a little skin on them, a few strands of cotton for hair. It was hard to believe she was going to live another minute. It had been months this way. I wanted to get in the bed, hold her, but I thought I might knock a tube out.

"Do you mind?" I said to Homeroom.

I locked the door and sat on the chair, the book. It was something about a process, a grief process. I guess the guy had been boning up.

"Hey, you," I said. My sister did a snort through her air mask, this noise like everything that had always been my sister was clotted and wet inside her and we might need a tool to scoop it out. I gathered up the covers, slipped my hand under her gown. I knuckled in down there. Her knees opened in her sleep. Her nipple went up. I pushed the tubes off, bit down.

"Hey, you," I said, into my teeth.

Sometimes when I tell this story to people, I say my sister

opened her eyes for a moment and our souls touched, my old soul and her pretty much dead one. I hope they don't believe it. My sister died a few hours later, but I was far away. I went to Peeptown. The place had really gone downhill. Then I found Gary and we went to the Jew-hater's bar. Gary had a bump nose and took the German's theories badly. Gary, I said, shut up and get a guitar. This place needed strummy music and maybe the hate would go away. I'd seen it happen, in other lives. Sandy was there, loaded, doing lap hustles for the dream of a bundle. Turned out Sandy was the bartender's daughter. Deirdre was her true name. We were together for years and years, here and there. I'm sure she was a whore in the time of Bismarck.

Her soul is older than mine.

Cremains

Here's Hilda with the big blind eyes. She hands me a letter on the landing.

"Can you read this to me?" says Hilda. "Can you say what it says?"

These old ladies, they stream out of their doorways in the mornings, they come stunned-looking to the hallway in their straw shoes. They stand around and wave me over. I'm the only able-bodied homebody here. The Super lives across the river and all the husbands are dead. The old ladies wave me over to do their dirty work. They must think I don't have any other kind, or maybe they figure I owe it to them to help. Not too long ago my mother was alive here among them, the youngest of the young of them by years. Now it's just me and the morphine my mother left in the morphine drawer. I haven't been down to the old streets in months. Once you've tasted the bounty of the pharmacy, who wants bad counts and bad people again?

"Tell me what it says," says Hilda.

"Rent is going up," I say, slap her phone bill in my palm. "Forty more bucks a month. Or you're out."

"Bastards," she says. "To an old blind lady."

"The times we live in," I say.

"We don't live in any times," says Hilda. "I hope I die soon. Will you read the paper to me?"

"Not today, Hilda."

"Your mother was a saint. She read the paper to me every day."

"How can she be a saint?" I say.

"Not that kind," says Hilda. "Why can't I just die?"

Hilda has a little fuzzy skull with lots of veinwork. It wouldn't take very much in the way of force to grant her this wish. It would be an act of mercy, maybe. I could go around to every door, ask who wants the service. I'd be a hero to some, to others just another doper with an old lady peeve. The newspaper Hilda gets delivered would call me evil. The one I buy on the corner would say it's more complicated than that.

I do lightbulbs for Mrs. Lizzari. She must run her lights all night. They say there's some kind of minuscule chance the whole thing will explode in your face, so I always turn away on the last twist. Don't mess with the minuscule, I say.

"Thank you, dear," says Mrs. Lizzari. "I can't get up on the chair like that anymore."

"No problem," I say.

"Don't hurt yourself."

"I won't."

"Be careful."

"I am."

There's some prison flick I saw where the cons rig the lights to fry a stoolie. It's just a flash, then he falls to his knees, his spine in a volted stutter. It always stuck with me, the way something does when you think it might pertain to you, a lesson to your kind.

"Do you want a cookie?" says Mrs. Lizzari.

"Thanks," I say.

"I brought these to your mother when she was in the hospital."

"These?"

"No, not these in particular. Cookies."

"Right."

"I took the bus there by myself. I didn't see you there."

"I was there."

"Well, not on that particular day."

I get down from the chair, chew my cookie.

"I saw Hilda this morning," I say.

"A sad case," says Mrs. Lizzari. "A sad case of a woman."

"She said she wants to die," I say.

"That's the oldest one in the book," says Mrs. Lizzari. "That's older than the book. And I know your mother taught you to keep your mouth shut to be eating a cookie."

My place is still pretty much my mother's place. I mean I haven't really moved any stuff around. I put up some postcards from my old girlfriend on the refrigerator, but that's about it. One of them is of a lobster, reads "Welcome to Idaho." This is the kind of humor that used to tide us over until we were high enough to suck each other off. I've taped it up as a testament to what's not really funny.

It's a hell of a deal to get a place like this in a city like this for next to nothing. The trade-off is doilies on the arms of the flower-print couch. I tried to take them off, but they were still somehow there, so I had to put them on again. This is why I haven't moved stuff around. It doesn't help. Even empty, your mother's apartment is your mother's apartment.

You just have to adjust.

My old girlfriend came to visit, and I could see she was uneasy. She'd never even known my mother and here were all the family photos in those accordion frames—the trip to Rome, NY, that day in the zoo with the spitting llama, the cousin with custard on his shirt. Here were doilies and cork coasters and sugarless sugar in a crystal bowl. My mother was of the generation that tended to tear up those little pink packets and pour them together.

I'm trying to keep tradition alive.

I got my old girlfriend to fuck me in my mother's bed, but we had to stop when she caught me watching us in my mother's mirror. It's a big mahogany-mounted thing with brushes and creams on the bureau beneath it. I could see everything in the mirror, the flush of us, the jimmying, and to keep from coming I tried to make out the labels on my mother's lotion jars: Cocoa Essence, Hibiscus Morning, Goddess Balm. Then my old girlfriend hopped off of me.

"I can't," she said. "That mirror. Too spooky."

"Fuck," I said, went to the bureau for some cream.

The old ladies here don't seem to understand. I may not have a job, but I work. I'm talking about dozens of projects well underway, with serious interest on both coasts, not to mention the midwestern markets. The ideas are tricky, though, so I have to make sure the times are right. That's assuming Hilda was wrong, that we do, in fact, live in times.

Whatever Mrs. Lizzari thinks, I visited my mother a lot. There just wasn't much to visit by the time I got on the scene. Lucky for me they had widescreen in the ward lounge. I restricted myself to several hours of television a day. You can get caught up in things, forget why you're there. You're supposed to be helping someone die, making it more reasonable with ice cream and gardening magazines. Next thing, you're glued to some cable premiere, *Who Were the Etruscans?*, *Captains of Vaccine.*

The hospital also had an in-house station. My mother's pain specialist had her own show. The episode on bone disease was great, though I can't say that Tessa, that was her name, was a natural. She was a little stiff, which I liked when she stood near my mother's bed in her dark dress with the lab coat on top, saying to my mother, "Let go, let go, let the angels take you now."

It just didn't work that well on TV.

When my mother started crying out for brands of candy bars they don't make anymore, we knew we were near the end. We held hands around the bed and Tessa lowered her eyes, started to invoke the celestial escorts again. I could see that my father, my mother's ex, had joined me in admiring throes apropos Tessa's ass. My sister caught this, shot me one of those looks she has mastered over the years, the one that says, "You pig, you're just like your pig father."

Withering, I think they call it, though the word takes on new meaning if you'd seen my mother that day.

It was hard to believe this was the same woman who once sat me down on the flower-print couch, said, "When you were born, they put you in a bubble for a while. It wasn't my decision. In those days the doctors were gods."

Now they're just priests, I guess, and my mother is maybe in a paradise of non-carcinogenic sugar substitutes, although her ashes, her cremains, as the undertaker called them, are tucked away in the linen closet. We can't think of a place to scatter them. Places never had much meaning for my mother. She liked people and things.

Those last days in the hospital Tessa slipped me a pamphlet on grief management. I must have missed that episode on the in-house station. The pamphlet advised the griever to shower frequently and treat himself to a fancy meal. It didn't mention doilies, but I may have an older edition.

It was also silent on the topic of the morphine drawer. My mother left a lot of dope behind. Also some syringes for the hormone she had to shoot. Her bones were doing a slow rot but she'd be damned if she got a habit. I guess I'm supposed to flush all these pills down the toilet now, but they tend to make my old-lady duties more bearable. Maybe it has something to do with my bubble days, but I've always needed something, just to do anything, or even to figure out what I need.

I promised my mother I would straighten out, but she was sort of in a coma. I don't think it counts.

Today I'm doing Hilda's dishes. I like to break one each time, so there's one less to do the next.

"Oooh!" she says. "That sounded like a saucer."

"Close," I say.

"A parfait glass?"

"No, think flatware."

We sit, after, for tea.

"When are you going to get a job?" says Hilda.

"What, are you my mother?"

"Your mother was a saint."

"I have a job," I say. "I'm freelance, self-employed."

"The bums are freelance, too," says Hilda.

"It's okay," I say, "I don't expect you to understand. Although, I must say, Mrs. Lizzari has been very supportive."

"She hated your mother," says Hilda.

"I don't believe that."

"Nobody believes anything anymore," says Hilda. "Why

would I make something like that up? By the way, did I tell you already that I want to die?"

"Yeah, you told me. But I don't believe it."

"Why would I make it up? What's the point of living? And the rent going up. They want me dead anyway."

"Your rent's not going up," I say.

"Well, it's not going down, either," says Hilda. "I'm done here. I can't even read. I love books and I can't read them."

"I'll read to you."

"Read what?"

"Books."

"I don't think so, dear. I don't really care for them. But one thing you could do for me is kill me. No one would know."

"I would know."

"You've done worse, I can tell by looking at you."

"You're blind, Hilda."

"I'm not blind to the world."

I'm not blind to it, either. There are all sorts of possibilities out there. You just have to be able to think sideways, is all. You have to know how to predict demand. My ideas are a bit subtle, and they may look funny on paper, but somebody's bound to bite. I've always been far-thinking. I could always listen to Top Forty radio and tell you which song would be a hit. Same thing with the Fall TV lineup. I know what the kids want, too. That's easy, though. It's just a crapshoot whether you get the colors and the chemicals right. But the old ladies who want to die, or have their lightbulbs switched, that's an untapped market. I'm living in a gold mine, or maybe a silver one.

Mrs. Lizzari comes to the door in her brassiere. It's the old kind, a severe network of clasps and fastenings, which is the new kind, if you pay attention to these things.

"Hey, Mrs. L.," I say. "Can you do me a favor?"

"Anything, honey."

"Can you fill out this consumer research survey I've worked up?"

"Oh, I don't think so."

"It shouldn't take you long at all."

"No, honey, I'm sorry. I'm on a government roll. I get money. I wouldn't want to anger anyone."

"No one will mind," I say.

"No, honey. Come back tomorrow. I'll have some more cookies."

Mrs. Lizzari closes the door before I can get a fix on the smell coming from her rooms. That's something right there. Old Lady Smell. You could market objects scented with it. A mild version. For the grievers.

Sometimes I take out my mother's cremains and set them on the dining room table. I keep them just the way the undertaker gave them to me, sealed in a cardboard box, cinched up in a velveteen sack. People like to call them ashes but it feels more like a couple of rocks, especially if you hold the whole thing in your hands, or swing it, as I do, on occasion, bolo-style from the sack cord. I'm still not sure why I do this, but it feels good, standing there in the dining room, windmilling my mother around.

One of these days we'll decide where to scatter her cremains. People say water is poetic but I think they just secretly like the convenience. Any creek or river has a little God in it. My mother's old neighborhood would be a good spot, but they bulldozed it for condos years ago. Besides, as I may have mentioned, she never seemed to care where she was, as long as the right people were around. The great sorrow of her life was that they tended not to be, and a sunshot vista, or a sparrow on the windowsill, this was no consolation.

Once she told me the story of the time a minor movie star was leaving a party and motioned her to join him in the elevator. She hesitated. The door shut.

"I was waiting for your father," she said. "He was in the can."

"That guy just wanted to fuck you," I said.

"How do you think anything beautiful begins?"

I'm a little worried about the morphine supply. I'd better get myself a crooked doctor or cancer soon. I'd better get myself a winning business plan or I'll be twitching the nights away on the flower-print couch.

Hilda hands me something in the hallway.

"Read it," she says.

"It says you've died, Hilda. Congratulations."

"Very funny."

"It's just your light bill. You should see Mrs. Lizzari's."

"She's afraid of the dark."

"Guess so."

"I'm not," says Hilda. "Know what I mean?"

"Listen," I say. "Let me ask you something. Say somebody, a messenger of mercy, maybe, was willing to put his freedom, or even his life, on the line, just to make sure yours ended in as quick and painless a manner possible. Would you be grateful? Would you arrange for payment, even? How bad do you want it, Hilda?"

"You're a sick boy. Your mother said you were a problem, but I always told her it was a phase."

"I thought it was, too," I say.

Mrs. Lizzari is down on the corner with her walker, her mesh grocery sacks.

"How're you fixed on light, Mrs. L.?"

"I'm a Broadway star up there!" she says.

Home, I boil some pasta and peas, fire up my mother's old Fischer radio. The youth of America sing their anthems of youth. Once I knew the words. I troll for soothing locutions, catch a familiar voice.

"Our culture is afraid of death, and considers it something we must wage a battle against. I say, surrender, submit. Go gentle. Terminal means terminal."

It's Tessa, I realize, even as the host breaks her off.

"Well, I guess you're saying just lie back and pray the Eastern religions are right about reincarnation."

"No, I'm saying just lie back."

Mrs. Lizzari calls me for a special batch, almond-ginger. When I get there she hands me a small canvas, lighthouse generica, a hammer and nails.

"Over the mantle, dear," she says.

"So, tell me," she says, hoisting her cookie tray, "what made you say those things to Hilda?"

"What things?"

"Horrible things."

"I was just trying to help."

"We don't need any help in that department, thank you."

When I leave I still have the hammer in my belt loop. I bang it on Hilda's door.

"Who's there?"

"It's your local service representative," I say, wave the hammer through the chained slit. "Whenever you're ready, Hilda. Just let me know. There's no reason you should suffer."

"Who's suffering?" she says.

You can hear them in the hallway, their early wheels. Mrs. Lizzari is in her house gown, helping the medics make the corner with their gurney. Hilda is up to her neck in sheet.

"She's okay, she's going to be okay," says Mrs. Lizzari. "She's not so lucky yet."

I nod, duck back inside.

My mother's windows get no dawn light, but there's a kind of slow undimming going on in the dining room.

I fetch the sack.

All it takes are the tiniest taps of the hammer to make a good part of my mother real old fashioned dust-to-dust-type dust. I crush a little morphine up and sift it in. I add some water, cook it all down in a spoon, draw it up through a hormone needle, roll my sleeve. I stanch the blood with velveteen.

Now I'm on the flower-print couch.

Now I'm thinking, is that the morphine, or is that my mother?

Something is setting beautiful fires up and down my spine.

The Morgue Rollers

Daddy can't stand the kikes. Daddy says they look down their kike noses at him in the state store, where Daddy picks and packs, crates up the Liquor Board liquor. The kikes treat him without time of day.

"Those fucking kikes," says Daddy.

Maybe Daddy's a little tippy tonight.

"You're tippy," says Mother.

"I stopped for a few."

"But Daddy," I say, "aren't we the kikes?"

"That's what they say," says Daddy. "I say it's them. Who needs them? Who needs her?"

What Daddy maybe means is that us Cherskys of the Hill District are not like the Blitzsteins of Squirrel Hill, except maybe my Aunt Rachel, who married in, and who we never see her anymore.

"Who needs her?" says Daddy. "Let her cavort with the kikes."

Cavort is a smartie word. It was on the vocab quiz. Maybe Daddy knows it because he used to be a smartie, too. Now he's sore arms, sore neck from him hauling all the Liquor Board crates, sore everything every night, aching, waiting for his salt bath, wanting to know from us which of us needs Rachel. Now he shushes up for in case the Old Lady will hear. The Old Lady is in her room with her high holy silver, the Chersky locket swinging on her collar lace. She never leaves her room. She gets her dinner after, and not the ham we hide away.

We are always shushing for in case the Old Lady puts her high holy ear to the keyhole. We never say the name of ham, or the name of Uncle Joey's Polish girl, Paula, Paula, Paula.

Let them hide the ham away. Let Daddy come home tippy, or call Uncle Joey a bum until Joey bawls how it's not his fault, it's the gas he got in France, the mustard. Then he'll peel off money for Daddy from his copper money clip. Mother says the money is green enough for legal tender, why ask what he does for it? A bagjob, a bet, a favor in a pinch? Bumhood is not Uncle Joey's fault, either. He gave his mustard mask to a boy with bad breathing. The gas came floating through the trees of France, and now he reads books all day, *Astronomy of the Gods*, *A Century of English Verse*, spits dip on the back stoop, gets mustard nervous, waits for the moon to be over the park for Paula.

Let us just be Cherskys, Aunt Rachel's Blitzstein shame. This is my belief.

Want to know my faith? School does. Mother says to say American.

"Hey," says Uncle Joey, "how about Alleghenian? That's what everyone around here is. Gypsy, dago, mick, it's all Alleghenian."

What about chink Chinese? I want to ask. What about my best girlfriend Mona Yee, who me and Mona are the front-desk smarties at Duquesne Grammar, tops, not counting Alvin Kwon? We are best friends with our shaved ices on the spit-brown stoop, and we are best friend rollers on our roller skates. Everyone who sees us sees us together, the Chersky girl, the pretty one, the only one, and Mona Yee, Chinese pretty. We are from up the Hill and we roll down it, past the bakery, the butcher shop, the state store where Daddy fetches whiskey for the kikes.

Sometimes I see Daddy through the window. He nods his curved-up jaw at Mr. Vance, the Liquor Board man. Maybe Daddy sees me but he never waves back. That's okay, it's like in school, somebody bombs you with an ink bomb on you, but even if the paper sticks to your blouse you better not turn, you better not look. Not if you want to stay a smartie. Only Alvin Kwon ever turns and only Alvin ever looks. He burns his eyes at the boys in back, the ones who vow they're sending Alvin to the Slabs.

"Never!" says Alvin, who's going to be mayor someday, and can recite the Gettysburg address in perfect Lincoln.

Today, Mona and me, we are after-class rollers, rolling under steel smoke, over all the broken sidewalk backs of mothers. We roll down the Hill past Paula's house, to the city pool, where I swim in the no-pee water. Mona is sweet and waits with her books on the lawn. The no-pee pool is no-Chinese. Mona doesn't mind. She's getting smarter while I do my crawl, my butterfly, my aqua-ballerina spins. Oh, if only there were more of us Chersky girls, spinning out the letter C, all of us identical, aqua-amazing in our no-pee ballet. Only after, when I'm dressing, do I remember Mona out there under the steel-smoke-lifted dark, under Paula's park moon. I come out with my hair knotty wet. We sit for another minute, then get ready to climb the Hill, skates laced around our necks. Mona's having ham at the Chersky's tonight.

Mother is mad at the Gypsies. What the Gypsies do is come to the back door, never the front door, ask to cut through. Who wants to tell a poor old Gypsy woman she can't cut through? Don't be a dummy, says Mother. Don't be a dingbat, foolish. Sure, let them through, but don't lead them. Otherwise, say good-bye to any silver on the table. Say good-bye to any nickels in a coin dish on the table.

"It's not their fault," says Uncle Joey. He's got ham-hiding eyes. His fork has the French shakes.

"Whose fault is it then?" says Daddy.

"It's their way," says Mother. "We teach our children to read, they teach theirs to cut through."

"My teacher taught me to read," says Daddy.

"Are you tippy?" says Mother.

"I'm fine. I stopped for a few. Vance was making a Federal case again, what do you want? You know, I should just join the goddamn army. Be useful. Maybe I'm old, but I could do something. Supplies."

"They'll supply you with the mustard," says Uncle Joey. "They'll get you good."

"Knock it off, Joseph," says Daddy. "And for the month, what have you got?"

Uncle Joey peels new bills from his copper clip. Mother says we know the money is U.S. mint and that's all we know. We don't ask. We're Cherskys, what's to ask? We all look over to Mona, as though to say, "Oh, Mona, sorry for the family fuss."

"Mona," says Daddy, "how's your ham?"

"Corned beef," says Uncle Joey, keyhole loud.

Tonight we will be secret night rollers, me and Mona, after the sink, the towel, the rack. Daddy goes to his newspaper chair, with all the war parts and funny parts of the newspaper we are not to touch. Uncle Joey tunes in the radio scores, shines his shoes for Paula. The way he rocks in the rocker when the college scores come on, the vein in his forehead pumping like a Frenched-up heart, you'd think he went to college, but everything Uncle Joey knows, Mother told me, he read on the stoop, spit into the wind.

It must have been a good day for bleacher blankets, all the college smarties with their cocoa and their cheers. The radio man calls out numbers over brass and whistles, drums. Uncle Joey jumps. He looks afraid, like they're going to supply him all over again, get him good, a gas bomb through the roof.

"Oh, shit, oh, shit," he says, and goes.

"Don't worry," I tell Mona, "he's just late to the park."

Mona and me, we sneak out the back and roll down to Paula's house, the alley window. Here's moonlight Paula in a wintergreen slip. Here's the bone-handled brush she pulls through her bone-colored hair. She brushes it and we wait for her to blow a kiss at Uncle Joey, who's wallet-sized, tilted with the post-cards in the mirror. He has his brim hat on, his over-the-shoulder belt, his going-off-to-the-mustard-war shirt. We have the same picture in our house, and one of Uncle Ferdie, who didn't get the mustard, who got a bullet in the neck instead.

Ferdie's buried under the trees of France.

"Blow a kiss, Paula," we whisper. But Paula runs her finger on the brush bone, lays it on the bureau top. The Allegheny stars are out over us, maybe the dipper, the bear, or all the god men Uncle Joey showed me in his star book, stuck there bawling in their sky robes.

We are night rollers rolling by the bakery, the butcher shop, down our block and down the Hill. We are rollers rolling past the houses like the Blitzstein house, where Rachel is so pinned-hair pretty, not a Chersky anymore, maybe with a locket on her collar, tearing tissue for the Temple Jews.

We roll by Mona's house, and Alvin's with the Chinese lights. "Alvin! Alvin!" we cry, but he must be busy burning up his mother's kitchen—liberty or death. When Alvin is mayor he'll emancipate Mona to swim in the no-pee pool.

We are rollers in the river town. We very much wish we could skate the black waters here. We roll on off state corners instead. Here are all the downtown buildings pointing steelish into the night. This must be where Mr. Vance will make his Federal Liquor Board case. Poor Daddy will have to join up for usefulness and maybe get a bullet in his neck. He'll be tippy in a brim hat in the sky. The Old Lady will die of holy silver sadness. Uncle Joey will marry in with Paula. He will tell us the truth about his copper money clip, the college scores. What about Mother, though? Who will bring her dinner after, after?

"Go, go, go," I tell Mona. It's a basement door propped open at the bottom of a stairwell. It's a dim, white light.

"Go, go," I tell Mona, but I go first, sideways, skatewise, down the stairs.

This dirty tile river was made for secret rollers. We are rolling down it, shushing ourselves as everything gets dirtier, dimmer, us wishing our wheels wouldn't click. We could get demerits. We could go to Juvey, even. The pretty Chersky girl in chains.

The hallway opens on a wide stone room.

It stinks of pickled animal, frog day at Duquesne.

"The Slabs," says Mona.

She skates off to the far dark behind us.

The dead men here don't look asleep. They look woken up into picklehood. They are stiff on cots that have skates fixed on. They are swelled up, blued-over, see-through, with black slits for bone to show. There are dead women, too, some the color of Mother, waxed over like hidden ham wax.

You don't have to touch to know how cold they are.

You don't need a clock to know how late it is.

Here comes a man in a dirty sky robe. He's pulling a cot with wheels across the stone.

"You here for this one?" the man says.

Even as I roll over I can see it, the copper money clip, there where the sheet doesn't reach. It's sticking out of Uncle Joey's shoe. "It's not his fault," I tell the man. "It's not. The boy had bad breathing. He couldn't breathe."

The man sweeps a hand for the whole stone room, all the slit-shot-caught-a-stroke dead, all the broken-back-mothers-of-dagos dead, all the mick dead and time-of-day dead and which-ones-are-the-kikes-kike dead, all the cut-through Gypsy dead, the kosher-paper-lady dead, the blued-over, see-through, Alleghenian steel-smoke dead, the college-drums-and-money-clip-we-don't-ask-where-the-bullet-came-from Chersky dead.

The man says, "Bad breathing, huh?"

The man says, "Looks like an epidemic to me."

I'M SLAVERING

Everybody wanted everything to be gleaming again, or maybe they just wanted their evening back. Everybody was from everywhere, had gathered here to hide from the daylight. Some of these people sat around a marble table with straws in their hands. It looked like they were waiting for lemonade. They were trying to get my friend Gary on the phone to get more lemonade. It was early, late, lockjaw hour.

"Is it like this in Geneva?" I said to a man at the table. I was new here, recommended to the straw people by Gary. I felt like the pupil of a great instructor out alone in the dead city.

"Is what like what?" he said.

"Is this like this?"

"I'm from Scarsdale," he said. "All I can tell you about is Zurich."

About then the woman with the telephone called out the terrible news.

"Gary's not anywhere," she said.

There were moans, whispers, ruminations on fate, hard words for God. People started to shuffle out of the room. A few fell on the coat pile in the corner.

"This is why I hate America," said the man from Scarsdale. "This brand of bullshit. Where the hell is Gary?"

"He told me he'd be over later," I said.

"That's exactly what I'm talking about," said the man. "And here comes the fucking sun."

The man bent his straw into a periscope, poked it over the windowsill.

"The sun, the sun," he said. "You fiery whore."

"Maybe I can find Gary," I said.

"You flame-blown bitch," he said.

"I think I know where Gary is," I said.

The man from Scarsdale spun his periscope.

"That's a good story," he said. "Work with that story."

I walked around the ruined sectors of the city and worked with that story.

It was really my story and it went like this: shaky, steady, shaky, steady. I was in shaky right now. I tended to waste a lot of time looking for Gary. It's difficult to stay the course to steadiness when you've got to find Gary all the time. It's difficult to do anything at all. Sometimes, when I needed money, I stole my girlfriend Molly's stuff, but the quality goods were running low. To top it off, I was pretty certain I was suffering from that deficit thing. That disorder. Everything flickered a lot, and I never knew which story I was working with.

Take the story of Gary's thumb. Many years ago, on the eve of manhood, Gary sawed it off with his father's Black & Decker table saw. Gave it to his mother on an olive dish, or maybe it was a cookie plate.

"You should have seen the look on my mother's face," said Gary, back from emergency.

The truth was, you could still see it on her a few days later, there in the bar mitzvah ballroom. That kind of look, it doesn't disappear, even with all that disco-nagila going, and Gary bouncing high in the chair. Gary's uncles, men with great bony mouths, slid Gary from his throne into my arms. I held him there, the bandaged hand between us, and under the din of Hebrew synths, I asked him why he did the sawing.

"They wouldn't let me watch TV," he said. "The late movie. Now I watch all hours. Anything I want."

That's the story how Gary left his thumb and his youth behind, though they did sew the dead thumb back on.

We had years as strangers before I saw him again, but somehow I've always been following Gary. What he did to his thumb made him, I believe, a wisdom-giver.

Me, I was never bar mitzvah'd. According to the tenets of my faith, I'm nothing close to a man, though I have a hairy neck and look older.

Walking around now I thought of all the times I used to walk around and see Gary on the streets of this city. It's funny to see someone down here from your town. You think everyone will stay behind and do everything you did all over again, forever. You picture old geezers in jean jackets doing whip-its behind the plaza.

But I got out and Gary got out. Everybody gets out. Getting out is not the problem.

You can picture what the problem is.

For instance, Gary tried to be a rock star, even trained his bad thumb to squeeze on a guitar pick, but rock was dead.

"Somebody should have mentioned something," he said.

Next thing, I see him loitering near trust-fund bistros, looking smug and hunted.

"I'm in goods and services," he said. "It's the only uncompromised medium left."

That was when I decided to buy his services, his goods. I was in a steady phase, but Molly was tired of my clarity. It's hard to fuck your girlfriend when she's fucked up and you're not. It's harder than the Skee-Ball they used to have at the Plaza arcade, all that agony over a fuzzy prize.

Now the sun was clearing the rooftops, the water towers. I thought of the man with the periscope. I looked for Gary in all of the Gary places, but I was too early. These places were all haunted by the future of Gary.

I wanted to score for the straw people, maybe make Gary proud.

I wanted to have friends from all over the world in the way of a man who has no friends. Maybe some of them were still heaped on the coats.

I went home when I knew Molly would be at work and started to pull her music off the shelves. This was what I called a mercy burgle, all those bands overmuch with faux hope for the world and untricky beats. I unloaded a stack of them on a British guy with a store down the block. He got by selling crap at a mark-up to club kids—used-up ideas, pants unpopular in their own time.

"I just staple a tag on and they buy it," he told me. "It helps that I'm a Limey."

The Brit's eyes had this pucker of awful witness. He'd been everywhere just as everything got ugly: art, philosophy, rugby, love. Maybe what he'd seen had made his teeth fall out, too.

I asked him if he knew where I could get what the straw people needed.

"I don't travel that road anymore," he said. "It's clogged with idiots like you. Now sod off."

He held a mug of tea and I noticed a sliver of cellophane floating on top. Was that the new dead style?

I went down to the park and watched the sparrows peck things off the blacktop. Those animal kingdom shows I always watched with Molly made like there were animal societies, but these birds just hopped around unbidden. I picked one sparrow to be the hero. He proved himself the moocher of the flock.

There was a man in Lycra on a nearby bench, breathing hard, a paper sign pinned to his chest.

"Race for the Cure," the sign said.

I went over to another bench and waited for a feel in the air that would mean the coming of Gary.

"I'm resting," said the racer. "I'm going to get up. Just give me a damn minute."

People always said that what Gary did to his thumb was due to a disturbance, but I figured it happened in a moment of calm. Once he sawed off his thumb and gave it to his mother on a breakfast tray, he was in the free and clear. Who would ever bother a boy like that again? Who would tell him when to go to bed?

This is what I mean by wisdom.

The death of rock was just bad luck.

But Gary was getting it together. Meanwhile, he was mentoring me. The last time I'd seen him he came over with his knapsack, dumped out pills, powders and plant kingdoms on the kitchen table. Molly was gone and I looked around for something of hers to give Gary.

"Hey, are you sure you can handle all this stuff?" he said, pinched a razor blade between his living finger and his dead thumb. "Look at you, you're slavering."

I asked Gary for some girlfriend advice.

"Do you love her?" said Gary.

"That's what I'm asking you," I told him. "Do I?"

He kept propping his thumb up against the side of the razor.

"Why don't you use the other hand?" I said.

"Give a man a fish," said Gary.

"You want fish?" I said.

Now Molly was home with her mortar, her pestle. She liked to crush things for wellness when enough was enough.

"You're home," I said.

I smelled fennel.

"I had a headache."

"I'm sorry," I said.

"So sorry you went and took more of my stuff? Don't tell me, you just need it for a little while."

"I need to find Gary," I said.

"You need a better embalmer," she said. "Look at you."

"Look at these," I said, spread out my hands for her, my thumbs. "These are all that separate us from the beasts of the field."

"What beasts?" said Molly.

"The ones of the field. In the field."

"Actually," said Molly, "that's a myth."

"Actually," I said.

"I mean," said Molly, "factually."

"If Gary calls," I said, "tell him I love you."

"Get the hell out of here," said Molly.

"Just give me a damn minute," I said.

I went to get some coffee, to think hard about where Gary

might be. But then I started to think hard about what Gary said about fish. Give a man one why?

There was a straw dispenser on the counter next to my coffee cup. You pushed a little lever and the straw jerked out.

I had a flitter, a flicker.

I saw Gary bouncing high in his ballroom chair. I saw him carried in it across the city, waving to crowds with his bandaged hand. His tusked uncles bore him across wide avenues full of birds. They took him into all of the Gary places, the parks, the bars, bodegas. Gary's mother and the Brit danced around the chair with feathered parasols. I was running to keep up. I had a message to deliver, memorized on some prior occasion. The message went: "I am running to keep up."

A hand poked out of the crowd and hooked my arm.

"Pay extra to nod on my counter," the coffee man said.

"I wasn't nodding," I said. "I was passing out. You want to work in this town you should learn the difference."

I paid for the coffee and headed off to the straw party. I pictured the man from Scarsdale watching me arrive through his periscope.

There were only a few coats left on the hallway floor when I got back. Through a doorway I saw some of the women on a bed. One slept with her tongue out in the other one. A phone glowed open in her hand.

I heard Gary in the next room, laughing with the man from Scarsdale. They looked to be lords of something fallen. There were white dunes and straws on the marble, pills and cash on the floor.

"This guy," said the man from Scarsdale, pointing. "He was here before. Who is he?"

"He's a rising young angler," said Gary.

"Come again?"

"Give a man a fish," said Gary.

"Ah, yes," said the man from Scarsdale. "Many applications to that little homily. Gary here has not yet taught me how to fish, so it's a good thing he finally came over. I was starting to do lint off the carpet again. Are you familiar with the fable of the dropped rock?"

"He knows all about it," said Gary, chopping, sifting.

"Hey," the man said to Gary, "what happened to your thumb? Did you break it?"

"Childhood accident," I called from the couch.

"Yeah," said Gary, "my mother misjudged me."

"Listen," I said, "I just saw this guy with a sign on his shirt. RACE FOR THE CURE, it said."

"Sucker," said the man from Scarsdale, stood.

"Where are you going?" said Gary.

"Me?" said the man from Scarsdale. "I'm going into the bedroom. I'm going to put some of this shit on my cock and slip it in those dyke asses before they know what hit them. Then I'm going to take some valium and fall into a deep, beautiful sleep filled with dreams of Geneva."

The man from Scarsdale winked at me, walked out of the room.

"Jesus," said Gary.

"Christ," I said.

"I mean, what is that?" said Gary. "What are we supposed to do with that?"

He stared into the mirror. His razor hand shook.

"Tell me what I'm supposed to do with that?" said Gary.

"It's okay," I said. "He's just some guy."

"I'm tired," said Gary. "I'm so tired."

"Everything's fine," I said. "You're here. I'm here. Everything's fine."

"Fuck here," said Gary. "We were from a town. A little town. Do you remember?"

"What a question," I said.

"There were people there," said Gary, "There were cars. Carports. You knew where to park."

"Dog hatches in the doors," I said. "Dog doors. Nearmont Avenue. The trestles on Main."

"Spartakill Road," said Gary. "Venus Drive. The Hobby Shop, the Pitch-n-Putt, Big Vin's Pizza, the Plaza."

"Behind the Plaza," I said.

"Exactly," said Gary. "Behind it."

We were quiet for a while.

"Evil's not one thing," said Gary. "They didn't teach us the gradients. We could have stayed."

"Blown our brains out in our cars," I said.

"Not me," said Gary. "What did he mean, Geneva?"

I got up, took the man from Scarsdale's seat, pressed Gary's dead thumb in my hand.

"Are you sorry you did it?" I said.

"Get the hell off me."

I stroked his thumb, brushed it, tenderly, the way you would a blind, tiny thing fresh-pulled from a hole.

"Just tell me if you're sorry," I said. "Because here we are. Because, me, I've been following you. Do you understand that? I've been following you all along. So, just tell me, are you sorry?"

"Hell, no," said Gary. "I wanted to watch TV. Anyway, what's done is done."

"Done and gone," I said.

"Don't fucking wallow," said Gary, and pulled his thumb away. "Never fucking wallow. You wallow, you're pretending you were something else in the first place. I know who I am. I'm Gary. I go down into the street, I'm Gary. I've never stopped being Gary. There's no cure for it. There's no race. It's not a race, okay? It's a contest. Do you get what I'm saying?"

"Yes," I said. "I'm with you."

He walked over to the window, a vista of sky, brick.

"Don't be with me," said Gary.

Admiral of the Swiss Navy

I can't remember the name of the camp. It was somewhere near a lake near Canada. I learned a good deal there that I would later rely upon when I threw away my youth. What I learned when I threw away my youth was crucial in my development as a misdirected man, so maybe it's all connected. What they say about character is true, though I can't quite remember what they say about it.

That summer we used to get stroke books for us to stroke ourselves with at bedtime. We used to get them from this trunk our counselor dragged between our cots.

"Dig in, faggots," he'd say.

We were all of us vicious getting to the good ones. We'd never seen stuff like this in our towns.

Some of us used to go smoke cigarettes behind the Port-O-Sans. Mr. Marv caught us one time, wanted to make a point. He was going to send us packing, which I guess is not a big deal looking back, but at the time it was seen as a stain. Plus to have your dad drive up in that sad kind of station wagon. What I did was give Mr. Marv some of the names he needed. I gave him the names of boys you've never heard of but who were known saboteurs of good camp citizenship. I'm not sorry I did it, either. If I saw those boys today, I'd say, "You brought it on yourselves."

I did see one of them in a coffee shop once. It's doubtful he made me. His eyes had the ebb of his liver in them and he bore the air of a man who looks right at you and only sees the last of himself.

"Don't worry," I told him. "You didn't miss anything that year. Except maybe Van Wort."

"Who are you?" he said.

"I'm the ghost of Van Wort," I said, and got out of there. There's no gain in having a fellow goner watch you order all-night eggs.

Van Wort was the fat kid who put our camp all over the local news that summer, and if you were localized near Canada and watching TV back then, you might have caught my debut. I was the one standing in the dining hall saying, "He brought it on himself."

I don't think I believed that, even then, but I guess I wanted to say something memorable, something beyond my years. I could have said what a terrible tragedy it all was, but Mr. Marv seemed to be in charge of that part.

Mr. Marv was probably of a type but I only ever knew him. He wore swim togs and parted his hair like a magician. They said he was a teacher of history in the winter somewhere. That summer, though, he was just Mr. Marv, blitzed at the bonfire, babbling on about the time he was a kid and sneaked into a ball game. He had come to see this DiMaggio take the field on bad feet. Bone spurs, Mr. Marv told us, ankle damage, the last of the brave.

What was he talking about, bone spurs?

What's so brave about that?

I slept next to Van Wort. I listened to the air whistle in and out of his fat chest. He said he had a chronic bronchial. He said it like a lie he made up a long time ago.

I watched them come to him night after night, boys with their mosquito sprays, their shampoos, tennis rackets and combs, warm water in toothbrush cups. Van Wort was fat and his name was Van Wort. With that combination, why would you pack your kid off to camp? Let him play with ladybugs in the safety of his own lawn.

The counselor with the stroke books tortured Van Wort, too. He was just a mean kid with more years on him, more muscles, a denser perm. He wore a spoon medallion. His name was Steve, or maybe Ivan, and his stroke trunk was deep. When we got through the first batch he hauled out some more. These were magazines that didn't even have real magazine names. They just said what was in them, the way creamed corn at the market just said creamed corn on the can.

Steve-Ivan called Van Wort Van Wort Hog. Or Fat Fucking Shit, for short. He was the one who told us to piss in Van Wort's canteen. It was the best canteen in the bunk, brand new, fuzzy wool, a cavalry sleeve. We took turns pissing in it and dipping it down in the Port-O-San hole. We left it under his short-sheeted bed.

When he found it his eyes went dark, his great arms started wibbling, wobbling on his knees. The canteen, he told us, was a gift from his dead father.

"It's just a joke you fat fucking shit," said Steve-Ivan. "We're your friends."

"Really?" said Van Wort. He looked as though he was ready to believe this, or wanted to be ready.

"Sure," said Steve-Ivan. "Just don't be a Van Wort Hog and run crying to Mr. Marv."

Van Wort stopped crying and he didn't run but he went to see Mr. Marv. Steve-Ivan was somebody's cousin near Canada, though. The whole thing blew, as they say, over.

I got damn good at boxball during this period. I was, if

you will, the boxball king. Maybe it's not crucial to the story of Van Wort, but I think people should know.

We did a camp-wide Capture-the-Flag. I wasn't in Van Wort's unit, but I can tell you things got pretty hairy out there. What happened to this one girl in the beet field was a shame. We never did know what the rules were, or which kids were still living or dead. My unit just marauded around. We laid waste to Mr. Marv's azaleas and tied a boy to the tetherball pole. Then we lucked into view of the flag, this dinky fluorescent thing like the kind for a sissy bar, planted on a hill. Mr. Marv was up there with some other campers.

"Don't let the heathens flank us, you curs!" we heard him shout.

We flanked them hard. We flew up along a ridge near the tennis courts. Van Wort appeared out of nowhere with a croquet mallet in his hands. Some of us batted the mallet away and beat Van Wort to the dirt. I led the rest of the unit on the resumed flanking maneuver. I didn't want to know what they were doing to Van Wort.

Mr. Marv noticed our wild charge a little too late.

I lowered my head, took flight.

"The day is lost!" he said, as I hit. "Our Lord has forsaken us for vile Moors!"

"Vile Moors," he kept saying, which I didn't get at the time, but I see now was because we had Black Sean with us and it was Black Sean who took the flag.

Then the agony of having your nuts crushed by an airborne boy, it must have suddenly arrived on Mr. Marv. The man shut up.

Victory equaled a sack of candy bars, to be divided evenly among all living members of our unit.

Van Wort spent the night in the infirmary, though a boy

who was there for a spider bite said there were no visible marks.

We played Freeze-Please every breakfast, lunch, and dinner. Steve-Ivan would say "Freeze, Please" while we were eating and we'd all go stone-cold statue. Whoever moved first was Admiral of the Swiss Navy, which meant you had to scrape and stack the dishes, bus them over to Black Sean's mother in the kitchen.

The Swiss have no navy, but who knew that then?

We called Van Wort the Commodore because he couldn't hold still. I think it was unfair, really, because it wasn't so much him as his fat that was moving, if that makes any sense at all. Study a fat kid hard and it might.

"Well, it looks like another lucky day for the Hog," Steve-Ivan said one morning.

"I'll help him," I said.

Everyone gawked, as though I'd been struck with sudden bolts of faggot lightning, but it was just this feeling I had, that Van Wort was getting a bad break.

He wasn't so off. He wasn't even weird. It wasn't like he wrote bird poems or wore the wrong kind of underwear.

"Why are you doing this?" said Van Wort.

"Just because."

"I don't care what you do to me," said Van Wort. "If it's a trick, it's a trick."

We were quiet and stacked for a while.

"So," I said, "who killed your dad?"

"Nobody killed him," said Van Wort. "He dropped dead. I saw it."

"No shit," I said. "You saw it?"

"He went blue and had a bubble on his mouth."

"What'd you do?"

"I didn't do anything."

"Didn't you give him mouth to mouth?"

"He had a bubble there."

Some of us were smoking behind the Port-O-Sans after lights out when Steve-Ivan wandered by. We had figured him for off to the bars on the highway by now.

"Hey, it's lights out," said Steve-Ivan.

"We know," I said.

"That means lights out out."

"I said we know," I said.

"Don't wise off to me," said Steve-Ivan. "You think you're special just because you've been going for those hog rides?"

This was wit near Canada. The boys did a round of barnyard jokes about me and Van Wort.

"So, what's it like, sucking on the bacon?" said Steve-Ivan.

They called me Bacon from then on.

I didn't mind the cracks, but I missed the camaraderie.

I calcified, got crusty. I lost my boxball crown.

Each night they came to his bed where he lay wheezing. It wasn't even foot powder and Indian burns anymore. They wanted to hurt him, to make him bleed. They taped him down to the bed frame, went at it with tweezers and pocket knives. They got his sock bunched up for a ball gag. They pinched off pieces of him with nail clippers and tiny sewing shears from kits their mothers had packed because it was on the list.

I'd get up and walk to the other end of the bunk until they were done.

In the morning I'd help him clean up, wipe down the blood until it was just dark nicks.

We talked about everything except what they did to him.

We talked about the day's activities, the boats, the beads, the weaving. We talked about our dreams the night before.

He told me he had gun dreams where the gun wouldn't shoot, falling dreams where he fell into a stilled river that had his father's face in its bed. He had one where all the girls at the girls' camp were rolled out on a float for his fancy. I told him he should keep a dream diary and he told me he did, showed me a spiral-bound notebook with his entries. It read:

Gun
Girls
River
River
River

He told me he had given the eulogy at his father's funeral, that it was easy, he'd just used an essay he'd written for school and substituted "my father" for "our founding fathers."

I started to admire Van Wort. But then I'd hate him for being so weak. He'd given up even the shrieking and they rarely bothered to gag him anymore.

"Why don't you fight back?" I said.

"What's the point?"

"The point is you show them you're not a pussy. Then they leave you alone." I believe I'd first heard this argument advanced by a talking beagle on one of those claymation shows the Lutherans used to produce.

"Will you help me?" he said.

"No," I said. "That would be wrong."

"Why?"

"It's complicated," I said.

Then it was the last day of camp. We packed all our stuff in duffels. Tomorrow we would strip our beds and get into our family wagons, wave.

At our last lunch Steve-Ivan said that Van Wort and I would be voted camp love-birds at the camp banquet that night.

"Vote us whatever the fuck you want," I said.

"Oh, you little bitch," said Steve-Ivan.

We had to stack without even a Freeze-Please and Van Wort wouldn't look at me.

"What's wrong with you?" I said.

"I'm done with this," said Van Wort.

I took that to mean that he was going to do something, make himself the last of the brave. What he meant, though, was that he was truly done. Van Wort took a canoe out to the middle of the lake. We were doing free swim and we heard him call to us, watched him drink from a big plastic jug and just sort of bend over, roll off the bow into the lake. You'd figure drowning would be hard going to begin with, all that lung smash and lung stove and no air to dream of rivers anymore, but picture it with your guts burning off from a stolen jug of kitchen lye. Steve-Ivan dove in to save him but Van Wort was too fat. We watched them bob together in the middle of the lake. Then Steve-Ivan was bobbing up and down alone. He swam back weeping, or maybe it was the water.

They got Van Wort's body out with a special boat. They had him in a strap swinging off the gunwale. His swim trunks trailed out from his feet and you could see all the night wounds on him.

"Self-mutilation," said Mr. Marv. "Interesting."

The news trucks drove up that afternoon.

Van Wort's father appeared, too. He was a skinny man in a sun hat. He stood on the shoreline shouting at no one in particular. I walked up to him.

"I'm Bacon," I said. "I was his friend."

"Were you his Judas, too?" said Mr. Van Wort. He busted me a tough one on the jaw. Then he took me to his bony chest.

"I didn't mean that," he said. "I know you were his friend. Bobby wrote me about you."

I had long forgotten Van Wort was also a Bobby, if I ever knew.

I wonder if his father saw me on the newscast that night.

"Friend of the Victim," they flashed across my heart.

I was voted Most Humane at the camp banquet. Black Sean was Leadership Qualities. His mother cried. Steve-Ivan got up with a God's Eye he claimed Van Wort had woven for him and Mr. Marv led us in a Moment of Silent Reflection.

Van Wort, Mr. Marv told us, had touched all of our lives.

He may have just been talking, like he did about the bone spurs, but he was also right. I put on a ton of weight in school that year, got jumped and beat in my town a lot. It felt good, like I was getting free of something, but I never let on that I was enjoying myself. Then I found a severe diet, sought welcome from a band of semi-evil people. We were all nearly beautiful and eager to destroy each other for it. I had the kind of time where you don't notice the time going by, but it did.

Ergo, Ice Pick

Someday, I shit you not, we are going to smash the state. We are going to smash it good. We've got time on our side. We are up in the hills with time on our side, and time's pal, history, is pulling for us, too. Martin says it, and I believe it. What's not to believe? What is to be done will be done.

Up here, we are so far from our old homes. We are so far from where inside our old homes are mothers and fathers and TV's to believe, shiny bars to hang towels from, bottles of things to wash our hair with and soften our shirts. We are far from the campus, too, where maybe I was out of my league, or maybe they were out of mine. Damn them, the ones on campus, and the ones in town. They walk around like everything is howdy-dory. They are blind to everything they cannot see. Soon as I heard about smashing the state, I was in. You don't have to convince me the smell I'm smelling is the stench of the state. Look around, sniff it—the coffee, the roses, the rot, the aroma.

Up here, we must beware. We are safer in the hills but we are not safe. The long arm of the law is bendy and long. All we can do is wait. We are waiting and we wait.

Some days, Martin and me, we shoot the shotgun over the landlord's roof. Some days we get in the truck, go four-by-four on the pond road when it ices, skitch it. Every day we cut the trees where they grow thick on the ridge. Martin cuts them and I haul the wood to the road. The landlord says to cut what we need for heat. The forest, it comes with the rent.

But we always cut more for barricades, for bonfire fuel.

The barricades are for the revolution, the bonfire fuel for bonfires, which the landlord forbids, that fucking kulak.

We like to skitch and we like to loaf, but we can only do it until Martin's wife Lucy comes home. Then we have to look busy. Lucy says the revolution, for revolutionists, is twenty-four-seven, but most days Lucy goes off in her blood-technician whites. Me and Martin, we drive out for a snack.

"Doing hillbilly shit is a good stress reliever," says Martin.

"Look at Trotsky and his opera," I say, "I mean Bronstein. Look at Bronstein."

We are watching our pie cool at White Power Pizza. White Power Pizza is also called Hank's, after Hank Krull, the owner, but if I say to Martin, after a long day of kulak-roof-buckshot-lofting, or pond-road skitching, or pond-ice sliding, "Hey, let's go to Hank's," he has no idea what I might mean, but if I say "White Power Pizza," we are four-by-four with all due speed.

We are watching our pie cool and feeling the coolness of glances from Hank and his White Power Pizza men. They are boys, really, fallen from football glory, with iron crosses on their floury arms, tiny tears inked under their eyes. Every pseudo-hillbilly in a fabric-softener-softened shirt knows the meaning of this cooling glance. It's the one that comes before the knuckle-dusters, the brickbats, the blackjacks, or those funny circle blades for slicing pies.

"What the hell are you looking at?" says Hank.

"Just watching a pro at work," Martin says.

"The key is to keep the ovens clean. They had a problem with that in Poland."

Hank winks, shoots us a little Nuremberg number with the flat of his hand.

Every revolutionist is a student of the odds, says Lucy, or

maybe Bronstein said it first. It's a truth every Bronstein better heed.

We abandon our perfect pie, hurry out to the truck. We drive back up the pond road, past the landlord's house. You can see her through the window with her sons, small and sandy-headed darlings, sitting like a family yuletide greeting while she reads to them from one of those big-assed animal toddler books, the kind where hippos lecture on democracy.

"Fucking kulak!" I scream, my voice lost to wind.

Brothers and sisters, we are compound-bound.

The compound is our little house off the forest road. I love our little house, the graveyard beside it, the woods all around. I love to stagger out and piss in graveyard snow. I stare up at the moonpie moon, or dream of the little girls buried at the treeline under crooked stones. They died of typhus in the age of Millard Fillmore, my favorite president from that special time when I had to memorize those ruffle-throated men. Maybe our house is haunted, but it only makes me love it more, the whine and shudder of floorboard and strut. It's all grained up with ghostliness. I love the iron hook I carry for the hauling of the wood that Martin cuts. It is hooked in my coat for readiness.

I love to play with the little minds of the sandy sons when they come over, curious.

Also, I love Tina, in my sleeping bag, up in the attic room. Good, sweet Tina with so much to give to the world and giving it to me, sleepytime hummers and wake-ups, too.

But don't get me wrong. Most of all I love the revolution. Maybe I'm just tired of the wait.

The landlord thinks we are communists. We are not communists. What could a kulak, with her damn hippos, know? Communists? Sure, there are some around, the next town over. We saw them once at White Power Pizza, dumber than fence-holes, yacking their excuses for Misters Stalin and Mao. Not us. We say forget it after Bronstein got it. A clusterfuck from then till now. That is our tendency, as Martin says.

Me, I tend to say, "Let's get the twelve gauge," or, "The pond road is totally iced. Let's ride."

Martin tends to need persuading. Martin tends to pour more coffee and talk about Bronstein. He loves the pointy-bearded man so much, he says his born name. Bronstein, Bronstein, Bronstein. Bronstein does Siberia, Bronstein smites the pesky Kronstadt sailors, Bronstein peers through learned spectacles into the dark tomorrow.

"Bronstein had Hitler pinned," says Martin. "He knew what was coming. He figured Stalin out, too. Ergo, ice pick."

I can't help but like the ice pick part. I can see the skullmeat in the garden.

There's a winter's worth of wood already, but we keep the maul and wedge out front with some scraps to whack at for when Lucy drives up. While we make our preparations, drink down our vodka-and-Gatorades near the scrap-whack part of the yard, the little kulak boys come over. They are miniature soldiers, future sausage casings of the pork apparatus. They sit smug on our stump chairs, as though they own them, which in the world as it is, as opposed to how it could be, they do. I throw a bag of shake and a packet of extra-wides into the lap of the older one.

"If you can roll it, you can smoke it," I say.

"I'm ten."

"Happy birthday," I say.

"It's not my birthday."

"Then happy nothing," I say

"Everywhere," says Martin, lowering the maul to the grass, "there are children younger and fiercer than you, ready to shuck the yoke of oppression."

"The yolk is too runny," says the smaller sandy son.

"That's the point, little man," I say.

"What's the hook for?"

"For the gruesome necessaries," I tell him.

"Mom says she's going to evict you." says the older son to Martin.

"Do you believe the hippos operate under false consciousness?"

"Mom said the university kicked you out because you were crazy, and your friend here because he was dumb."

"Don't you see the crisis built into late hippo capitalism?" says Martin. "There's nothing idealistic about it. It's fucking math."

"Don't curse-word me," says the boy. He hands the shake and papers to his smaller kulak brother.

"Take this to Mom," he says. The other boy speeds off through trees.

"You're in deepies now," says the older sandy son. "Mom said one more little thing and she was calling Hank Krull."

The boy walks the snowholes of his running brother, a mittened form between the bends of birch.

"Deepies," Martin says. "Don't tell Lucy. Don't tell her a thing."

Some days we're up there smoking on the prayer rock off the hill trail, smoking on the big slab facing east. Martin says the local braves used to sit here a few hundred years ago to watch the sun go up, watch the wagons roll by, beseech the Great Spirit to kick Manifest Destiny's ass.

"But the only way to win," says Martin, "is to organize people."

"What people?" I say, wave out to the half-stump woods.

"They're coming over tonight."

"Tina, too?" I say.

Tina is my lady of the revolution. She was a daughter of Midwest mansions, come to university to study slides of the paintings that hung in her father's halls.

Then she took Martin's elective, "Introduction to Resistance: Semiotic to Semi-automatic," and he saw in her the makings of a revolutionist. This was just before the graduate-school dean kicked Martin out for "beliefs antithetical to the pursuit of happiness."

Martin took Tina home to the compound, to Lucy and me. We ate rabbit cassoulet. It was Martin's specialty. We drank a case of beer, then laid into some good port. For the sake of function I had given up shooting speed.

Tina came upstairs to see my Kronstadt, to kiss it.

"Martin really loves you, you know." she said.

There are certain reasons why women tell you of another man's love for you, but I did not know them then.

"Pledge allegiance to me," I said.

"Martin says we will eat in communal kitchens," she said. "Thousands at a time. Everyone will work three days a week. No surplus."

"We'll get married in a tank," I said. "We'll win over the army and they'll give us a tank. A Bradley Fighting Vehicle."

"Forget it," said Tina. "When the state withers away so will monogamy and marriage. Good riddance. Besides, I've only been with four men so far. Only one without rubbers."

"Anyone I know?"

"Martin thinks the house is bugged. Do you think so?"

"Assume surveillance, rest assured," I said, quoting my mentor.

We are scrap-whacking in the yard, all business, when Lucy drives up. She gives us her don't-we-have-enough-wood look, cluckety-cluck.

"Don't even," says Martin. "It's been a long day."

"A long day of what is the question," says Lucy. She can be sitcom mom when she isn't technician-white lady, or Rosy-Lucy Luxemburg.

"Oh, Lucy," says Martin.

"Crazy bitch," I say.

"Hey," says Martin. "Watch it."

"In a good way," I say.

Martin does some whacking. He always lets me slide, slither out from what I say. Maybe he feels guilty, being my teacher once, and me still a little slow. Maybe it's our fabric-softener softened shirts. We are from the same kind of towns. We both know the sound of swivel-head spray at midnight on a summer lawn. We both know the weak secrets of us.

"Bronstein came from a farm-owning family, you know," says Martin.

"About the ice pick incident," I say. "Was he wearing his glasses?"

"Every day with you. Enough."

Maybe he's right. Maybe it's being in the hills like this, with people down in town doing good and evil, and us just having to wait.

When Martin brought me here to meet Lucy I knew from the first moment that there was something between us. Call it chemical, call it mineral. It's vegetable when she is out in the garden in her morning robe, picking radishes for dinner. Somehow, though, without even a kiss, I suddenly became their son, the sulky one, the wild one, all the ones they vowed to never bear.

I made peace with my lust as a matter of priority.

Lucy is our rock, our reason.

Martin is the teacher, but it's Lucy who will set us free.

Still, the meals the man cooks! My God, if he were not the Bronstein of his age, he could have gone to New York City, been master chef to the ruling class.

"The idle's aproned idol," Martin said.

Tonight is Greek night, lasagna.

"A popular peasant dish," says Martin.

Lucy drinks off her wine.

"I couldn't find this poor woman's vein today. They give you three tries, then someone else takes over."

"You'll feel better at the bonfire meeting," says Martin.

"Tina's coming over with some new recruits," I say.

Lucy lifts up the wine bottle as though to examine the label. It's the usual vineyard scene, happy serfs up to their hips in grape.

"Christ, how did this happen to me?" she says. "I tell them about all this at work and they think you should be committed."

"What did I say about that?" says Martin. "At work, you never heard of me."

Lucy bangs the bottle on the table edge. In the biopic of Lucy it will break, but now it only bounces.

"I'm going to kill someone," she says.

"That's silly," says Martin. "For now, I mean. It's anarchic, futile. We must build a base of—"

"Fuck your futility," says Lucy. "I'm going to fire a bullet into somebody's ear."

"That's nice talk for a nurse," says Martin.

"I'm a blood technician, my dear. I have a job. Did you get this month's check from mommy yet? You're thirty fucking years old. And your little moron friend here. Can't decide whether he wants to do you or me."

It hurts, but I forgive each sentence before the next hisses out.

"You know," says Martin slowly, "Bronstein did not rise out of destitution, either. It's not a requirement. Would you rather my mother give the money to the Policeman's Benevolence Association?"

"Fuck Bronstein," says Lucy. "I'd waste him with an ice pick in half a second."

"You need a nap," says Martin. "But first, how about a little surprise?"

"I'll get it," I say, go to the kitchen for the key lime pie.

The new recruits drive up in a rusted sedan, a classic suburban bougiemobile, the kind my father used to drive me around in to show off all those atrocities of the state, the natural man-made wonders that always have those splintery benches nearby to drink warm root beer on. Put a quarter in the bughead metal scopes and maybe you can see the blood of workers drip-dried on the dam walls.

They pile out, girl after girl, stringy hair, parkas and hats, bundled, fevery sweetnesses who believe what I believe.

Here comes Tina with her deathmarch boots and mansion-colored hair, a deep-tongued angel like a painting from before Mister Marx was born. Sometimes when I see her I worry our cause is real, that we will die in low rooms with buckets and wires and sponges. State men will spaz me with volts, goad me into informancy. I have a low treachery threshold. Then the hummer days will be a faraway dream.

There are some new boys here, too, the kind who read French in the original and trick you into thinking their hearts are pure. These types prey like mantises on the kind and curious. There is one named Floyd I have seen doing deep stares at my Tina. It may be time for a cadre-to-cadre chat.

Lucy feeds the fire with our busy scraps. We lean into the light and say our names.

"Greetings from the campus branch," says one boy, so gallant with a zit-scorched chin. I raise my beer to him.

"Smash the state!" calls a sweetness, and giggles, as though goosed by the dark.

"Welcome all," says Martin. "Tonight is a special night for me. It is exactly ten years since I came to the conclusion that human life makes sense only insofar as it is lived in servitude to the infinite. You may ask what I mean by that. Look around you. See the moon? The outline of the trees against the night? Is that what I mean by infinite? Well, I could cut those trees down tomorrow. I probably will. I could detonate the moon. That's not what I mean by infinite. Certainly we are not infinite. We are flesh and blood, minds full of the rot of capitalism. Born dead, really. No, comrades, what I mean by infinite is..."

Now comes a tender kind of animal squeal from off behind the woodpile. I know it, that sound, know it too well, and my heart frogs up. I find her there with that boy, Floyd. She is doing what she is doing as though it were some kind of contest where you have to be quick and cannot spill.

"Traitor!" I say.

"You don't own me," says Tina, "I belong to history, you dumb fuck."

"Hello, comrade," grins pinned Floyd.

My hook is up, hooked in the moon, but I cannot move, cannot take my eyes off the kid's majestic thing. It's like the first time I read Nietzsche, and Martin had to talk me down.

Now Martin talks me down once more. My hook, too.

"It's okay," he says, "it's okay. Go back to the house. Go back to the house, man."

Now I must be shouting. Martin's hand is on my mouth. Now I must be biting. His knee on my neck.

That night I dream of sirens, the deep, womby wail of them slicing over trees, Lucy screaming, "Barricades! Barricades!"

It's a two-pronged attack, what they call a pince-nez in tactical circles. Cherrytops roll off the pond road onto the compound, crunching ice. That kulak bitch trails them in her jeep, calling out the window, "Get those communists! Get those junkie creeps!"

"We are not communists!" I call out in my world-historical dream-world voice, which is deep and resonates with the inexorable.

Through the flames of the bonfire I see forms of men come through the birch line. They hop stumps and scrapwood, sweatshirts and facepaint caught in the hack of headlight beams.

They have baseball bats and compound bows. Pistols squawk in the graveyard and the far-off woods. Rape shrieks come down from the prayer rock. The flower of our nation lies in puppet mounds around the fire pit.

There is Martin in a bloom of ruin among them.

I awake, peek out the attic window. The bonfire is an ash disk on the lawn.

I listen to Martin and Lucy, their Saturday morning coffee talk, or what slivers of it slat through my floor.

"I'm just worried that he's really crazy."

"What do you mean?"

"Just that. That something's really off."

"I know."

"We should call his folks. Or maybe contact the psychiatric community, problematic as that may be."

"Is this all the cream?"

"Take mine."

"You know, I love you in that robe."

"We're not done talking about this, Martin. I'm going to call his folks. I think he's snapped. He tried to kill Floyd."

"He seems a little wiggy. I shouldn't have given him that hook."

"He smokes all of our pot."

"He doesn't really do much for international socialism."

"Those things I said, I was angry."

"I've been selfish."

"Come here."

Lucy hands me a stack of newspapers on the way out to my father's car.

"Onward, upward," she says.

We drive down the pond road.

"Well," says my father, "I hope your little adventure in social unrest is over."

"Guess so," I say.

"When the freaks turn you out, then it's time to re-evaluate things. Wouldn't you agree?"

"You have a point."

We pass the kulak's house, turn onto the country road, go by White Power Pizza one last time.

"Hungry?" says my father.

"I'll eat tomorrow," I say.

Home is so fabricked and glowing. I had almost forgotten the softness of the world. Here's my little room, the bed, the desk, the lamp, and my little mother in it, folding towels for me.

I am down in the valley now.

I eat many tomorrows away. I miss Martin's cuisine. Everything here comes in plastic with a scissor line. I watch the men on TV in their good, dark suits, their free-market starch. Lucy would be laughing, Martin cursing, but I can only stare.

My mother and father say they see a leap for the good in me. I am quiet and take my boots off at the door.

I think of Tina often. I think of her in several fixed positions, with slight rotation.

Someday, I shit you not, the order will come down. Someone will surely be sending the orders down then. There will be a knock on the door, an old comrade in the glittering tracksuit of the new regime, chin pimples gone to grave divots. The state, he will explain, the new, glorious state, requires assistance with a certain hero of the people who has lost himself to rogue notions. We need a man, he will tell me, a man who can get in close, a man who is maybe a bit soft in the head but with a terrible hardness to him from all his short-term memory loss.

This order will come down and I will slip my hook in a grip for the road. I will take a slow bus up to the hills. We'll sit there up on the prayer rock, Martin and me, talk of our victory, recall old struggles, laugh about the sandy sons. It will be a meeting of dearest friends and I will fill his bong for him from my private government stock. We will weep for Lucy, slain at the Battle of the Malls. We will mourn Floyd, him of huge heart and member, executed live via satellite, purged by fiends. We will rue those dark forces of counter-revolution and counter-counter-revolution that maneuver as we speak. We will sigh, admire the layers of light in the sky from the sunset behind us, build a fire for the cold coming night. I will hoist my hook from the grip, kept all these years, a memento of exile, of sacrifice.

"Hey," Martin will say, "I've been looking all over for that fucking thing."

"Forgive me, Bronsteins!" I will shout, hook my hook in my hero's eye, drag him by the brow bone to his pyre.

Beautiful Game

Gary gets to pick a park. A nice gesture on the part of the state. Or is it the city? Gary studies the list, picks one far from home. Last thing he needs is a neighbor, a friend, family even, seeing him in some kind of get-up, coveralls, a neoprene vest, poking around with one of those trash-poke sticks.

The kids from the school, say, with their frisbees, their dogs.

It would get around.

It's hard enough this woman at the desk knows what he's done. Maybe she's from a bootstrap family, foreign. Here's Gary, lucky to be born a citizen, wasting his good fortune. All he can do now is try to set things straight.

He'll start with the park.

He has some days before he's supposed to report. He stays home, drinks O'Doul's, shoots cocaine, watches the tube. It's non-alcoholic, the O'Doul's. Gary bought a case of it by mistake. They don't mark things properly anymore. Still, it'd be wrong to pour it down the sink.

They have a tournament on TV, football, the other kind, countries, flags. He finds a team to follow, a side, Cameroon. So far, a Cinderella story, the color man says. But how does Cinderella end? Does she win? Gary hopes so. Something will happen to him if Cameroon loses. Maybe it's stupid, reminds him of all the stupid people he always thought himself positioned against, but here he is: a rooter. It is not a good epoch for position-taking. How long is an epoch? Maybe he can wait it out.

He goes out at sundown, after the games, buys some bagels, cigarettes. This morning's bagels marked down. A man stands near the bagel store. His legs are in leggings. Blanket strips? He's bleeding from the mouth.

"They took my teeth!" the man says.

"They're just getting started," says Gary, gives the man a buck.

At the bank machine, Gary doesn't check his balance. Better to leave it to the gods. Someday the machine will shun him. Why know when?

Gary had a band back when that was a good idea, toured the basements of Europe in a bus. The Dutch dug it best. The Dutch got the put-on underneath the hurt, the howl. Gary's not sure he would get it himself anymore. This was years ago, before the whole thing got big, and small again. Now it's gone. The tradition is gone. The kids at the school, they hardly even know that really famous group, the one with the singer who killed himself. The singer in Gary's band killed himself, too.

The drummer quit, went to divinity school.

Now Gary likes to tell people at parties how he works with kids. It explains him, his shoes, his age. The only parties he goes to are those his mother gives. He talks to the children of his mother's friends, younger people, yoga, the big new job, no stains on their teeth. He doesn't really work with kids, either. He works near them, odd jobs, errands, the elevator, recess guard. The kids wave, say his name. Kids are precious, priceless.

Gary has a price.

He just lowers it a lot.

The thing is, all Gary did was try to stick up for the cart guy. Sweet guy, cart outside the synagogue, always the freshest stuff: squash, cucumbers, fruit. The older cop was hassling him, the rookie hanging back.

"Officer," said Gary to the rookie, "what's this about? A permit?"

"Fuck off."

Gary was uptown to meet someone, a buyer. A tiny deal, a taste, a favor, bagel money while school was out. The buyer was nowhere.

"I pay your salary, officer," said Gary.

"I doubt it, pal."

The older cop banged the cart guy down on a tomato crate. The cart guy was talking in a bootstrap tongue.

"Hey, Turkey, you from Turkey?" said the older cop. Gary eyed the gun on his hip.

Maybe it was a test from God, see if Gary would stick up for the cart guy.

Maybe it was that Gary once played a little football, American. Tactics, crackback, spear.

He put his hand on the shoulder of the older cop.

"Lay off of him," said Gary.

Clothesline, clip.

Gary was on his belly, cuffed. The rookie was in his pockets. "Well, well, what have we got here, Mr. Solid-Fucking-Tax-Paying-Salary-Payer Prick?"

Lock-up was winos unzipping, pissing on the walls. A boy Gary knew from a bulletproof bodega crawled under a bench and slept. There were dozens of them there in one cell. Hands cuffed at their bellies, they filed out for bologna on bread. He befriended a French kid, a student, busted in some club, a ketamine sweep. The French kid was here on a grant to study business. Catch you with K in Tokyo, the French kid said, and they do a number on you with a sword. Or maybe it was Malaysia. Either way, it was no time to be a student.

One guy, he went for a fit, a seizure, right there on the cell floor. The rest of them stood around, hands clasped together like a prayer meet. Smart guy, thought Gary. Get yourself a bed, warm food. The guards figured him for a fake, though. They were not dumb men, not for here. They kicked the faker in the buttocks, the back. The French kid nudged Gary, said something in French.

They got juice, more sandwiches. Gary gave the French kid a look. He was sorry about the cheese, American cheese, jail cheese, the whole thing.

"How did I ever get here?" said Gary.

"A big van," someone called out.

They led him through some corridors, took him before the judge. It felt like early evening but there was little in the way of evidence. There was a box painted on the courtroom tiles. "Defendant Stand Here" was painted in the box. A short man, maybe hoping to pass his dark sneakers off as shoes, pinched Gary's arm.

"Just tell me, did you do it?"

"Do what?"

"That's what I thought."

The defender faced the judge, said something in English. Felonies, misdemeanors, mitigations. The prosecutor, handsome in a good tan suit, spoke the same words in a different order. Gary tried to follow the exchange but he was beat.

He could smell the stink coming up from his boots.

The judge rubbed his gavel.

The bailiff buried his key in Gary's cuffs.

A woman at a window handed Gary a carbon receipt. It listed what the cops had taken from him at the station house, laces, a lighter, some lip balm, a pen. He waited for her to slide his things across the counter in a big envelope. Probably manila. He had a constitutional right to his lip balm back. He waited a while.

"Get out of here," she said.

Fucking Cameroon. Why can't they concentrate? They pound the ball upfield, get an open net, shoot wide into the stands. Their captain looks much older, slaps them around. It does no good. Their coach, a Croatian, walks the sideline in a windbreaker. Gary gets out his atlas, looks up Cameroon. Symbols for goods and resources, coffee, oil, lumber.

The Cameroon captain goes up for a header. The ball slants in for a goal.

"The glass slipper continues to fit!" the color man says.

But wouldn't the glass shatter with the girl's first step?

Gary goes to the kitchen for another O'Doul's. When the O'Doul's runs out, he'll get some real beer, but right now there's a principle at stake.

Gary's mother calls Gary.

"Are you coming to my thing on Saturday, Saturday afternoon? It's for Mrs. Lily's daughter, Lorraine. She just got her masters in social work. It's a little gathering. You two will have a lot to talk about with your job and all. Oh, and her mother says Lorraine's a big fan of your music."

"I don't make music anymore," says Gary.

"You know what I mean. How are you, honey? You sound a little blue. Are you blue? Did you find any summer work?"

"Maybe. It might start Saturday."

"Really? Saturday? Doing what?"

"A city job, with kids."

"Great, Gary. That's great. But please try to get out of it for Saturday. I'll give you the day's pay. I really want you to come to my party. I really want you to say hi to Lorraine."

"I'll try," says Gary.

"Try and make it more than try," says his mother.

Gary had a feeling his best friend was going to blow his head off, but what are you going to do? The guy had always said that suicide was the plan. He said it the way some people mention the possibility of law school, vague and determined at the same time. Those people usually did go to law school. They saw themselves as lawyers all along. This guy just happened to see himself as dead.

Divinity school, though, that surprised him. It wasn't that the drummer seemed godless, just kind of vapid, dumb. Gary got offers from other bands, but only the minor, imitative ones. It would have been like playing in his own tribute group.

Gary figures he'll be fine when he gets over the idea of devotion. There was that morning in Rotterdam a man and a woman got down on their knees in the street. They took him up to their room, gave him dope to smoke, played his music for him as though this time he would hear it anew. The man pulled tablature of Gary's songs from a cold oven, his file drawer.

"Your band is one of those bands," the man said, "in a few years, forget it. Legends. People will see, separate the wheat from the chafe."

"What about now?" said Gary. "And you mean chaff."

"Now is different story," the man said. "There is still a lot of chafe."

Besides, he's sick of rock. He likes kids. He's shooting a lot of cocaine, sure, but that's just because he's off for the summer. This bust, though, it bothers him. Community service? What community? The cop and the cart guy? The man with no teeth? This city is just a lot of brickwork and stonework and people bearing down on nothing at all.

He remembers the last time he saw Lorraine Lily, a few winters ago. A tag-along, sweet, with tits. Maybe he could knock off the death trip, get clean, get clear, with Lorraine. Benefit from her training.

"Last licks," he says out loud, pulls the plunger back, eases the needle home.

Neuron, axon, penalty kick.

Now the Africans are leaping into each others' arms, sobbing, falling to the field, grabbing the turf.

"This carriage isn't going to turn into a pumpkin anytime soon, I'll tell you that," the color man says. "In years to come we're going to look back on this. This moment will become legend."

"What I hope," says another announcer, "is that moments like this will help promote international brotherhood through the majesty of the athletic endeavor."

"Well put," says the color man, "and well-hoped. But let us not forget that this is just a game."

"But a hell of a game!"

"The beautiful game. You can see why from the slums of the far-away slums to the war-torn fields of warring lands, this is the world at play."

"So simple, yet so complex."

"A dance and a battle in one."

"You fucking idiots!" Gary says to the screen, but it feels forced, as though he is just some man watching TV.

Maybe Lorraine is religious, thinks Gary, the inner roar of his ears on the wane. I could learn the words. I could sing of God.

There is one last O'Doul's.

One day Gary chaperoned a field trip to the city's science library. The kids unpacked their knapsacks and set to work. Gary loitered in the stacks, found a book about barbed wire. It had sketches of every variety, maybe named for the rancher who first knotted it that way. Scutt's Clip. Corsicana Clip. Brotherton Barb. He thought he could do something with this, something creative, but he didn't know what. Maybe a song with all the names of barbed wire in it. It would be good not to explain.

There was one boy in his charge they said might be trouble. It was a private school, so no one ever put it quite like that. What they said was that Vernon was a genius.

Now the boy sat alone at a silver table.

"Hey, man," said Gary. "What's wrong?"

"My homework," said Vernon. "My fucking homework. I don't want to do it right now."

"I know where you're coming from," said Gary.

"Sure," said Vernon.

"No, really," said Gary.

"I bet you couldn't even do my homework."

"It's not about whether I can do your homework. It's about a feeling."

"What a pile. Look at you. You're not even a real

teacher. What happened to you? I bet you're over twenty."

"I'm thirty-one."

"See," said Vernon. "If I'm anything like you at your age I'm going to kill myself. What do you think of that?"

"I think you ought to save yourself the hassle and do it now," said Gary. "I was at a faculty meeting and your name came up. Turns out you're not a genius, after all."

"Liar," said Vernon, but his voice wavered, and in a moment he was crying. Gary went back to his book. He felt terrible but harbored a secret hope that this moment would count for the genius as a minor scar. Someday Vernon would be accepting a prize at some institute and self-doubt would flare up in the guise of Gary, leering.

They are waiting for him at the park station uptown. He sees the trash sticks leaned up in a bucket. A woman ranger in a tight uniform leads him to a bench where some others sit. There are reams of flyers and boxes of envelopes piled on the floor. The flyers announce a summer program for kids, nature walks, rollerblading, marine biology by the lake.

"Are you still hiring for this?" says Gary, holding the flyer up.

"Oh, good," says the ranger, "I was worried we wouldn't have a comedian today."

"No, really," says Gary, "I'm qualified."

"Fold," says the ranger.

The others are younger than Gary, not white. Kids from nearby.

"You got a car?" says one of them, who has announced himself as Junebug.

"No," says Gary.

"Well, if you did, what car would you get? A Lexus, right?"

"A Gremlin," says Gary.

"A what?"

"It's a cool car," says Gary. "Like in a fucked-up way."

"Gremlin? What'd you do, anyway?"

Gary tells them about the cart guy, the tomato crate, the cop. He doesn't mention the cocaine.

"Hey," says Junebug to the ranger, "Qualified Gremlin here threw down with a cop."

"Well, he better not try any of that shit with me," says the ranger. "I'll put my foot in his ass."

They fold flyers until noon, break, fold again.

"What about the garbage?" says Gary, finally. "Shouldn't I go out into the park with one of those sticks?"

"Why, looking for a weapon?" says the ranger. She gives Gary a mop and points him to the toilet. The seats are gummed, the tiles caked with boot tracks.

"When it sparkles, you can go," she says.

Gary sees the man with the leggings outside the bagel store.

"How're the teeth?" calls Gary.

"What?"

"The teeth?"

"Look," says the man, moves in, as though about to show Gary his mouth. "I'm not *your* homeless. Got it, fucker?"

Gary goes up to his place for a clean shirt. When he comes back down the man is sitting on a grate, cinching a seabag.

"No hard feelings," the man says.

Gary holds out a buck and the man waves him off.

"I have other offers on the table right now," the man says.

The bus is packed going over the bridge. Gary presses his head on the tinted window. He stopped at the bank on the way to the bus. The gods of the machine have wearied of him. The buyers are off at their bungalows, yoga retreats. He will have to borrow some money from his mother again.

It's hot on the bus and everyone wears short sleeves except for Gary. He picks at the few tiny flecks of blood on his shirt with his fingernail.

Gary's mother hugs him at the door.

"You look like you got some sun today. Out with the kids?"

"Yeah."

His mother hooks him on his arm's tender spot, guides him across the room. A group is gathered near the bay window, pouring whiskey.

"Boy, am I glad you came." Today his mother has that almost dazed expression which, along with the featherings at her mouth, people take for mirth. "These people are drips. Put on any music you like."

"I'm fine, Mom," says Gary.

"Hey, there's Jacob Gelb," says his mother. "Remember him?"

Gary looks at the man, tall and tan, easy with his body in casual silk. Gary has that flicker of thought that comes along with his mother's house: I wonder if I'll turn out like him when I grow up. But Gelb is a few years younger. Gary remembers once putting worms in his hair, or firing an air pellet at his nuts, something senseless and maybe not forgotten.

"A drink?" says Gary's mother.

"Just water."

"Good for you."

Gelb keeps a plastic cup aloft with his foot, his loafer. A woman sways down near him in a goalie pose, dangles her fingers out.

"Hey, Jake," Gary calls. "Been watching the Cup? How about that Cameroon?"

Gelb looks up without missing a tap.

"Those guys are gone. Knocked out this morning, or last night, or whatever. My money's on the Netherlands. The Goudas."

Gelb kicks the cup into the fire place, throws his arms up, mugs, mimes the frenzy of thousands.

"I'd trade it all in for one good run at goal," says Gelb. "When I have to go to Europe for work I just order up food and watch the leagues."

"So cosmopolitan," says the woman. "Going to a foreign country to watch sports on TV."

"I go to make money. I watch sports to clear my head."

"Same here," says Gary.

"You're Gary," says the woman. " I'm Lorraine. I heard what happened to your friend. I'm sorry."

"Thanks."

"I've never heard your music, but people say it's really interesting."

"Oh," says Gary. "I'm not playing anymore, anyway."

"What are you doing?"

"Working with kids. Disadvantaged."

"Wow, that's great," says Lorraine.

Gary tells her all about his little brothers Vernon and Junebug, their eventful day in the park, the nature walks, the craft hour. They talk for a while, mutual friends, traumas of youth. Lorraine writes Gary's number in a day book stuffed with business cards.

"I'm going to call you," she says. "I want to call you."

"That would be great," says Gary.

A few days later she does. Gary is poking around for a vein. The vein is always right next to where you think it is. You have to dig hard. Work hard, dig hard. The blood dries in jagged curves around his arm, his wrist. Scutt's clip.

Lorraine leaves a long message with several numbers at the end of it. He is going to call her back, tell her he needs to go away for a while, get well, but his well-hoped hope is that she will wait for him. There is something special there between them. It's hard to see, but it's there. The proof that it's there is that you can't quite see it.

Now, crowd sounds.

Dutchmen kiss the pitch.

The Drury Girl

"Do you want to see it?" said my father.

"Okay," I said.

"It's a beaut," said my father. "You should see it."

"Okay," I said.

My father gathered up his gown.

"Look at that stitchwork."

I looked at the bruises, the blood flecks, the sewn line of the cut.

"Look," he said. "That's where they took them."

"I'm looking," I said.

My father got sick on our sofa for a while. Sick man's beard, slippers, ripped robe. Bad days, he slung my old beach bucket in his belt to puke in.

Most days were bad days.

Old buddies chalked him up to dead.

Cousins, clients, called the house to mourn the loss.

His firm sent my mother a cheese wedge, a condolence card, but my father was not dead, he was sick, in the kitchen, sipping broth from a china cup. I brought him a spoon.

"Hey," he said, "did you check your people today? Check them every day. Be attentive. Unnatural swelling, that's what you're looking for."

"Okay," I said.

He laid his spoon down.

"I'm going to drink this soup from the cup," he said. "But that doesn't mean you can."

"Okay," I said.

"Stop saying 'okay,'" said my father. "Enliven your vocabulary."

"I will," I said.

Some days my father would dress, necktie, pressed shirt, take his coffee near the window. He'd do the jokes, the numbers, the eyeball-soaker, the sock-tucker, the suicidal Swede.

"What's for dinner, sweetheart? Asparagus? Ka-Boom!"

One morning he took his parka down from a hook, wheedled himself out over the walkway ice. He got his old Plymouth going. Dark exhaust gusted over the trunk and veiled it. Through the smoke I saw her, the neighbor's daughter, the Drury girl, come down Venus Drive. She walked our yard in a snow-colored quilt, bare calves popping out of boot fur, sleep knots in her hair. She walked towards us with her arms crossed, a vexed diva, shot white breath from her teeth.

"Nathalie's going to watch you while we're gone," said my mother.

"A babysitter," I said.

"No, you're too old for a babysitter. Just don't give her any trouble. Your father's not up for any trouble."

"Okay," I said.

My mother rubbed her knuckle on my spine. Our secret touch. The Drury girl slipped past us into our house, spotted my old bucket, held it up.

"Are you playing beach?" she said.

My father said I was his little helper but mostly I just hid. There he was, on the sofa, or in the fall-away chair. Sometimes, cartoon mornings, I found him sleeping with my bucket in his lap, a thin gruel on his chin. Once, his robe fallen open, I studied his wounds for a while. The stitches were gone, some of the hair grown back. The skin braided down to a wattle, a flap.

"What?" said my father, waking. "What are you looking at?"

"Nothing," I said. "I'm sorry."

"What are you sorry for?" said my father.

"I don't know," I said.

"You know what the situation is, don't you? You understand this, right?"

"Yes."

"Did you check your people today? Check your people, kid. What happens is they swell up on you. Sort of thrilling at first, but don't be fooled."

"Okay," I said.

"I was a fool," said my father.

Days they drove away for his injections, Nathalie stayed here with me, lit joints, my father's stash, spun the stereo dial.

"Crap," she said. "Tripe."

She wore T-shirts with the names of bands in spatters of blood, or maybe her night gown if duty called before noon. She was skinny, beginning to be rounded in the same places as the women on TV, the ones I called up like flip cards lying on my belly in the dark. The blonde widow on the Florida yacht. The space lady with the thimble in her ear.

"Do you like music?" Nathalie said.

I showed her my only record, a collection of gunslinger ballads sung by a man in cowhide who looked like my Uncle Sy.

"You'll learn," she said.

"Learn what?"

"How to dance and how to fuck. You want to dance?"

We danced, a tour of eras, tango, pogo, slide-and-dip.

"You're terrible," she said. "You'll never make it."

"Make what?" I said

"Good point," she said, "but answer me this: What do you want to be when you have to be something?"

"An astronaut," I said.

"Bullshit. Who taught you to say that?"

"President."

"Crooks."

"A rock star," I said.

"That's more like it."

Now we heard the door, saw my mother shove my father through it. He was weeping. He was wiping vomit from his beard with a dirty mitten.

Then it was a miracle week, a miracle month, a month from God. My father said he was on the mend. He got what my mother called his color back. My father said he was on the uptick, fit for light duty, maybe.

"I'm either getting better or I'm already dead."

The bucket went back to the shed with the diggers and spades. Breakfast, he did the disappearing-lip trick, the joke about the Pope, the Jew, the parachute.

He hung back near the coffee pot and palmed his patched head.

"What are you doing these days?" said my father.

"Fractions."

"I'm half the man I used to be," he said, or maybe sang.

I found him later at the dining room table, his glasses low on his nose, papers, pens, strewn.

"I've missed a lot of homework," he said.

I stood near him with my mother when the firm called with the news.

"Perfectly understandable," he said into the receiver. "No, the package is generous."

Done talking, he put the phone down, gently. He sighed, kicked a hole in the wall. He limped off to the fall-away chair and sat there, alive, destroyed.

He smoked a cigarette.

"May they all get cancer," he said.

I checked myself in bed each night. I kneaded my people. I turned on my belly, burrowed down and in. Somewhere between the mattress and me was Nathalie, the Drury girl.

Sometimes I would see myself walking up Venus Drive, the dream version, the houses steeper, the birch boughs soft with moth rot. I'd eye the berm for what they took from my father, skinned and glimmering in the leaves.

The Drury girl was drying her hair. She'd showered. I'd stood outside the door. She'd caught me, beckoned me in, let me watch her slide her jeans on underneath her bath towel. Now we sat on the sofa with our dilemmas, my fractions, her dangerous men.

"Fuck it," she said. "I don't care what my father says, I'm really into Keith Puruzzi."

"What does your father say?"

"Fuck my father. Which I'm sure would be swell by him.

Mr. Eyeball. What a prick. Oh fuck, I shouldn't talk like this."

"You always do," I said.

"I know I do. How's your dad? Not so good, right?"

"He's on the uptick."

"The what?

"The mend."

"They took his thing off, right?"

"I don't know."

"You've seen it, right?"

"Not . . . no . . ." I said.

"Your old man," she said, "he hid his pot on me."

Then it was still winter. The miracles worked in slow reverse. Wine into water into walkway ice. They were pumping him with what he called the hard stuff. He wore a watchman's cap and we gathered his hair from the sofa, the sink. My mother bought him a bigger bucket. It looked industrial.

"Don't worry," he told me, "I'll be dead soon, but not before I've ascertained whether you've cleaned your room. So don't think you can just wait it out."

"Please, God, stop that," said my mother.

"Stop what?" said my father. "Who are you talking to?"

I played with my Tonka dump truck. It was their gift to me for not wanting anything, for behaving, being quiet, remote. I was too old for it. I was remote anyway.

My father heaved. Sour sheets of air rushed out.

The Drury girl said we could make a surprise for my mother and father. They were due home in an hour. She dug around in her bag.

"Strip," she said.

The Drury girl had a rubber stamp, an ink pad sunk in tin. She inked the stamp and took my arm, laid the cut rubber on it. "John A. Drury," it read. "Notary Public."

She said for me to shut my eyes.

"Why are we doing this?" I said.

"You want to be a rock star, right? This is it. The show of shows."

"This is it?"

We rehearsed for a while.

"Wait," she said. "One more thing."

Now she reached down and took me in her fingers, twisted it a little, let it spring back of its own accord. She cupped her hand under, pinched, stretched, pressed the stamp in, let the flap pop back.

"Now you're perfect," she said. "Look."

She spun me to the mirror. I was measled in her father's ink.

We heard the Plymouth in the street.

"Hide," said the Drury girl. "Don't do it until I call your name."

I hid behind the fall-away chair. I listened for noises I knew, galoshes, boots, the slash and saw of winter nylon. Here came the voice of him, the old voice, from before the stitches, the bucket, the braid. It carried over the frozen world. My mother's voice stabbed at his pauses. These old rhythms of them, the tilt of happy talk.

They stood at the threshold, flushed, bundled things.

"Good news!" my mother said.

"Hold your horses," said my father. "They're not positive. They have to run more tests. But things are looking up."

"More than up," said my mother. "More than up."

"We'll see," said my father, and laughed. "But, yeah, sure,

maybe. Why not? Now where's the little beast? Where is he? I want to see my boy. I'm going to take him somewhere. You hear that? We're going to do something fun. Soon. You hear me? Where is he?"

I kept my crouch.

"Wait," said the Drury girl, "I know where he is."

The room filled with violins, static, saxophones, more static, more violins. There was a burst now, a hissing, gouts of feedback, guitar.

I eeled out from behind the chair, hips rolling, arms up, all of me thrown forward with whatever idea I had now of dancing. It was the Drury girl's steps and more, some lewd concourse of the blowzy slides my mother favored and the neatened twirls of bandstand teens. I shook my ass at them, shook my inked ass at my mother, my father, and then, with some kind of stricken pivot, I flippered my tiny dick. It was dreamlike only in that I felt seized with secret logic. Time moved in the real, my body bucked in it, all these parts of me pocked with the public seal of our good neighbor. The Drury girl receded, as though stunned by consequence, easing toward flight. My mother wore her school-play face. I could sense annihilation underneath. My finale was confected from the Tonka toy. Thrusting upward, I held the truck out, glided my balls over the painted bed.

"Look!" I said to my father. "These are my people! Are you looking? Are you looking?"

"Stop!" my father shouted, almost the cry of a bullied child. He bolted from the room.

I felled myself, with theater, head down, arms out, the vaudevillian's good-night wings.

The room got quiet. The Drury girl was gone.

My mother's galoshes, rimed, wet, leaked on the carpet.

"Okay," she said. "Okay, now."

We could hear my father moving with steady violence in the kitchen.

"We know that wasn't you," said my mother. "Was that you?"

"Who?" I said.

My father lived and I lived. We live still. Later, years later, my mother died. I have her galoshes, with my bucket, in a box somewhere.

The Drury girl, we heard, got work at the town plaza. Sometimes I'd watch her run our strip of yard to the street, to a car revving there, to a boy at rest in his Naugahyde bounty, that great godly twitch of electric guitar when she opened his door, her roaring off from all that was lived here or near us.

Probe to the Negative

Lucky for me I get a Larry tonight. Maybe he's a wandering daddy Larry, all alone in the middle of lonely places somewhere. I run the screens, tug him through his ache. Probe to the negative, that's what the training guide says. Poll, poll, poll, until you get a no. You're golden when they don't say no. You've gone to demo heaven. A Larry, though, is someone who is maybe lying. You can feel him through the wire. He wants to qualify. He wants to flee with you, wherever, away.

This Larry, he says, "Yes."

Says, "Yes, yes, yes." To work, to daddyhood. It's a survey about the schools and we need family men, solid citizens, taxpayers, debt-payers, payers in kind. Lucky for me the Larry checks out. Now we can voyage together across the vast spectrum of human experience: Excellent, Fair, Good, Poor, I Don't Know.

Choose, please.

"Good," says the Larry, "good, excellent, fair, good."

He never says, "Poor."

He never says, "I don't know."

"How many kids did you say you have?" I say.

"Kids?" says the Larry.

"This only counts if you have kids."

"The old lady has them. That's why I'm out here. It's me and the trees. My children are the trees, the sky. From where I stand, I can assfuck the moon."

"Thank you for your time, sir," I say.

"Thank me for my time! Thank me for my time! You think I don't know what you're trying to do to me? You goddamn mothership Jew!"

"You've been a real gentleman, sir."

Here comes Frank the Fink, my monitor, all mission control with his clipboard, his headpiece. Maybe Frank was a decent guy once, but he's management now. He sits with the other monitors at the edge of the room, eavesdrops, takes notes on our etiquette. Sometimes one of them will come over to your port with a personality tip.

"Start with hello," they'll say.

Frank lays off, though. I guess he thinks I would take it the wrong way, but I figure with a job like this, the higher you move up, the more of a tragedy you are.

"Hey," says Frank. "Forget that nut. You'll get a complete tonight, I can feel it."

"Thanks, Frank," I say.

Fuck off, Fink, I think, which is my thought of the day. I like to have one, it's almost Buddhist. Yesterday's thought was how did I get here, thirty-one, thirty-two, just this huge knot of unknowing and losing my hair. Big deal, you say. Male pattern baldness. But that's the thing. There's no pattern to it.

My last good thought was weeks ago and it wasn't even a thought. It was a building I passed on the way to Cups. Limestone, or maybe soapstone, with gargoyle guys on the sills. Homunculi, maybe, if that's the kind with the smirk. This was a building I knew from when I vaguely lived with a woman in it. She was fresh off the malls upstate, hungry to hurt herself. She wanted to write a history of art. She taught me all about Courbet and in return I went to Cups for both of us. Then she found some sculpture dealer's dealer, high-end guy, come to your house with a leather bag, a book in German. Now the girl and I, we had nothing in common anymore.

It's a bittersweet story, I guess. I wish I could remember more of it. She used to shoot too much cocaine and jerk around in her chair. It sounds bad, but if you'd been there it just might have charmed you somehow.

It charmed me. I even made some art of my own when I was with her. I took all the beat bags I'd copped—corn starch, baby powder—and glued them to some Belgian linen. "The Decline of Quality Control," I called it. The dealer's dealer dismissed it outright. He said it was an "insufficient interrogation of authenticity." I said I wasn't about to waste the real stuff. The point is, I shouldn't have bothered with that idiot. I had ideas in those days. I had hair.

It was Carla who started calling them that, Lonely Larrys, the ones who stay on the line. We used to share smokes on break. She's not around much these days. Maybe she's on a different shift. Maybe something better came along. That would be a shame.

The guy that hired me, he gave me this look when he gave me the job.

"You're hired," he said, "but it seems like a waste of a fine college education."

These days there's a conspiracy against the overqualified. I told him I was a painter, in the manner of Courbet, Corvette. He seemed appeased.

Tonight, everyone is telling me to go to hell. One guy I call wants my name, my real name.

"Saltine," I say. "Leonard Saltine."

He's going to report me to the bureau of something or

other, make a phone call to vent about a phone call. I guess these are the vengeful types. They don't believe in market research. They are enemies of progress. They want to go back to that dark time when America didn't care what kind of donut you liked.

"Saltine?" he says. "Bullshit."

"My name is nobody," I tell him.

"Yeah, I read that book, too," he says. "Well, I've got two eyes, pal."

"What book?" I say.

Later, I'm a few screens in with a lady from Duluth. Cough drops. Mentholated. Do they soothe? Do they soothe you to the poor, to the fair, to the good?

"These are dumb questions," the lady says.

"I didn't write them, Ma'am. I'm just doing my job."

I savor the saying of Ma'am. We never got to say it growing up in my town. People would take you for crazy, a peeper, or trying to burn them on school chocolate. Now when I say Ma'am I belong to a great tapestry of Ma'am-sayers stretched across the republic. We're just doing our job.

I get another guy, Wyoming, I think, one question to go. A country number comes over the line, a song about a jet pilot chasing Jesus through the sky, his heart on target lock. I ask Wyoming to rate the service at his local self-serve salad bar.

"Fair-to-good," he says.

"I need you to pick one, sir."

"How's about good, then? Good's better for you, right?"

"It's all the same to me."

"You pick," the man says.

"Okay," I say, "how about good?"

"Good's good."

Frank's up over me, doing his fink looks at my screen.

"Lose him," says Frank.

"It's complete," I say.

"It's compromised. You fed him a response."

"Don't do this to me," I say.

"Take a break," says Frank.

"Fuck you, Fink," I say.

I guess Frank has been briefed in the latest management techniques, because instead of hauling off on me, he smiles, rubs my neck.

"Okay, fuck me," he says softly. "Fuck me, and take a break."

The smoke room, it's just a stock room with no stock. It's concrete with a window in it. You can see the high floors of a brokerage house across the way. The brokers work late in their cubes, ties down, cuffs rolled, lips quickening against their headset mikes. We are all cold-callers now.

It's kind of dark in here but I can see her, Carla, her knees up on the heater. She's got these wide pretty shins gone to stubble. There's something about that. There's something about everything. Take her hair, tucked inside her sweater. We could be home somewhere, her legs, her shins, up in my lap. Those stiff little shoots.

We wouldn't have to tell each other about our days. It would be the same day.

"Hey," I say. "Got a cigarette?"

"No," says Carla. "Got any completes?"

"You?"

"No. But I got this one Larry, I couldn't tell if he was putting me on. Said he used to be a lion tamer. Used to stick his head in lion mouths. He said they always doped the cats, but still, you never knew when, well…"

"I never get a Larry that good," I say, lay my hand on her shin. I stroke down with the grain.

"This is a very troubling development," says Carla.

"I love your shins, you know," I say.

"No, I didn't know that. I wish I didn't know that. Now I have to wear pants to work. Don't ever follow me in here again."

I clock out early, turn my headset in, flip Frank a secret double bird on the way out the door. I call my friend Gary from the street. He's got a futon for me nights I need it, nights I sleep.

"This is Gary," says Gary's answering machine.

"Gary," I say, "this is me."

Down at Cups, the lookout hooks my arm.

"Big man, get me a bag of D, will you? I can't leave my post."

Maybe it's the way he says post that sways me. Now I'm part of an operation, a cause.

They call it Cups because you walk down a hallway of tile shards and wait for paper Dixies to come down on box twine. There's a kid I know from somewhere waiting ahead of me, but neither of us speaks. What is there to say?

I put money in the cup marked "D" and watch it shimmy up into the dark. It comes back down with one bag in it. Lookout's out of luck, I guess.

He's waiting out on the stoop for me.

"Well?" he says.

"Talk to your man," I say. "He screwed me. I paid for two and he only gave me one."

"Give them to me," he says.

"What them?" I say.

"Them is two bags. I gave you twenty bucks."

"Ten," I say.

Cups, it appears, also maintains a radical management style. The lookout puts a pistol to my neck and walks me back up through the door.

"Now," he says, "Why don't you say that again?"

"Oh, forget it," I say, "just kill me."

"What?"

"You heard me."

"Just kill you?" says the lookout. "You make it sound like nothing. What, you coming back? You got roundtrip? Frequent flyer?"

He hits me with the pistol, takes my wallet, leaves me the bag.

"It's good tonight," he says.

Justice has always been swift, and just, at Cups.

When I get to Gary's the girl from the gargoyle building opens the door.

"What are you doing here?" I say.

The girl lets me in, brings gauze for the dent in my head.

"I'm staying here for a few days," she says. "Gary's out of town, his aunt, his somebody, died."

"What happened to your place?"

"Couldn't make rent."

The girl and I sit in Gary's kitchen. She's got spoons, water, powders, works. It's like your only cozy memory falling out of the sky for you. I tie her off and hit her clean, the way I always could. She has veins like little tadpoles darting under her skin but I still know which way they're going. Me, I've got this hole in my arm like a great, dark lake. I just have to squirt the stuff in. The girl starts jerking in her chair. I clinch her down around the knees.

"Listen," I say. "I talked to this guy tonight. He was a lion tamer. Stuck his head in lion mouths."

"I could never do that," she says. "I could never tempt fate that way."

The girl twitches hard, almost out of her seat.

"Yeah, no reason to tempt fate," I say. "Like tonight, I asked a guy to kill me tonight."

"I can understand that," she says. "You can't do everything yourself."

When her spell breaks we shoot more of everything and sip something grape. We talk about old times, those nights in her bed behind the stone homunculi.

"What's wrong with your hair?" she says.

"I'm going bald," I say.

"That's not it. It's something else."

"What you're noting," I say, "is a dearth of pattern."

I kiss her, slip my hand under her ass and lift. She's about as heavy as a phone book. I lower her down on the futon and slide up to her hair.

"No," she says. "I don't feel like it."

"How do you know what you feel?" I say.

Now she peels down my fly, starts doing frantic things with her hands, annoyed, severe, like someone who forgot to defrost the meat. I can't feel anything but the view is exciting. I stick my fingers in her mouth and pry it open.

"Don't bite," I say, straddle her head.

"God save the circus," she says.

When the girl passes into what passes for dreams for people like us, I go down into the din of the avenue. I walk through the lights to the darker places. There's no moon in the sky to violate, no mothership, no hover of coming dominion. There's just the city, jerking in its concrete seat. Maybe I'm sorry to leave the girl up there, but if I stay she'll probably leave me. Then I'll surely be a Larry. I'll pace a room with the phone in my hand, eager to please some invisible slave. Good, I will say, excellent, excellent, excellent. I will never say poor. I will never say I don't know.

Every Larry who wants to live is a liar.

The Wrong Arm

There were marks in it, divots in it, a feathering of weals and burns. These were all the scars from all the times something tried to kill her in that arm. The stove tried to kill her. The cleaver tried to kill her. The brillo nearly did it, too.

Winter, she hid the wrong arm in her home sweater. Summer was bees and bad nails in the porch door. We were worried about summer, until it was summer and we forgot to be worried anymore. We packed all the food we needed in the plaid bag, sandwiches and sandwich stuff and twist-off cups of lemon pop, packed it up and drove away. She sat up front, packed in her proper place, beside our father, wrong arm pressed against the window glass.

We were going to see the boats. The boats of the world were sailing up some river.

I wondered what the wrong arm looked like to the drivers driving by. I wondered if they saw its wrongness spread there on the window, the burnt part, the brillo'd part, the cleaver'd.

All we knew about the wrong arm was that it was wrong to touch it, to pinch it, to rub it. Any other part of her was there for us to hold. The wrong arm was not for us to take her by and lead her. The wrong arm was not for us to tap it for her to turn.

The wrong arm would never heal right. That's why everything knew to try and kill her there. If harmed, our father told us, the wrong arm could be the end of her. He said end of her as though he meant no harm.

Our father told us about that man who died from how his mother dipped him in a river.

He had a wrong heel.

I figured I'd take the heel over the arm any day. This was given my pick. This was given if they let me pick, not just given being given what you got. Our father said sometimes you had to deal with the cards life dealt you, but I knew games where you got new ones. Lantern men granted wishes, too. I wanted to be the kind of boy who would wish the wrong arm wasn't wrong anymore. I was worried I was the kind of boy who wouldn't waste a wish.

My brother, my sister, we did not behave on the way to the boats. Some of us had to piss. The car needed gas. The pipe in the gas-place bathroom almost killed her. Maybe it was filled with boiling piss. We got back on the road to the boats.

There would be bees out where the boats of the world were sailing, but our father said you couldn't be scared of everything, or you might as well be dead.

"It's nothing to worry about," she said to us. "I've had worse than bees." She lifted the wrong arm a little where it stuck to the window.

What could be worse than bees?

Maybe wasps were worse. Maybe porch-door nails that could stick you with sickness even if your arm was right. Maybe porch-screen teeth where it was ripped and curled and our father never fixed it. Why didn't he fix it? Wasn't he summer worried, at least in winter? The bees were asleep then. There had been time. Who was I to say it, though? Me, who wouldn't waste a wish.

My brother, my sister, they had their parts of the seat, to

eat sandwiches on, to sing. Each of them was nothing to me. Everything that was everything was in front of me. My father was in front of me on the other side of the car. She was in front of me with just the seat between us. The wrong arm pressed through the secret slot between the seat and the door. It was our slot. I could see the blister from the hot-piss pipe. The arm would flutter whenever the road went hard.

We stopped to sit at a picnic bench, to take a picture of us, with trees.

The bench was bad with splinters.

I walked the clear and hunted for hornets. I hunted for ticks. I counted all the things that could kill her here. A piece of bottle, a broken comb. A thorn, even. No lantern man would ever let you wish it all away at once. You could only do it one at a time, and you'd never get it all. You'd just waste your wishes that way.

"What about here?" she said to my father.

"Not yet, not here," my father said.

Now we were on the river road. We spotted mast tips over the river hills. The plaid bag was on the floor. I was the keeper of it now. I put my hand in to feel the sandwich wax. I heard my father talking to her under the brother-and-sister songs.

He said, "One fucking opinion."

He said, "Don't think that way."

He said, "A specialist in New Paltz."

He said, "Don't think you're getting away from me yet."

He said, "We have to tell them. That's the whole point. Who cares about the boats?"

I was beginning to care about the boats.

I was beginning to be someone who wanted to see what

kind of boats the world had sent to sail here. I wanted that to be the point.

I started to ask a lot of questions about the boats. I didn't think it was wrong to ask.

Our father said the boats would be big and from every sea-going land. He said sea-going as though he meant some harm. He said the boats were one thing, and there was also another thing we would all have to talk about when we got to the boats.

I said I had some things I wanted to talk about, too. I said I wanted to know why they boiled piss at the gas station, what purpose did it serve. I said I wanted to know why he didn't just fix the porch screen while the bees were sleeping. I said I wanted to know if there was an Old Paltz, too.

"You shouldn't eavesdrop," she said. "We'll tell you everything."

I asked why the wrong arm was so wrong, whether what we were going to talk about was an even wronger wrongness.

"Look," she said, "the boats."

My father pulled the car onto a high plain, a meadow. The plaid bag slid when we braked.

We got out of the car and stood in the grass. We stood in our places from the car. People sat on blankets and bed sheets, pointed at the boats.

"Look," said my father, and we were looking.

"Does this answer any of your questions?" he said to me.

"Some," I said.

The wrong arm was backways in front of me like it was still in our secret slot. There were scars, blisters, sun peels, stains. There were birthmarks and marks from after being born. It could be anybody's arm, I thought. We were making it wrong by saying it was wrong. We should be holding it and rubbing it and taking her by it to lead her somewhere. To lead her by it to the boats. We didn't need a lantern man's one fucking opinion in New Paltz to make my mother's wrong arm right again. We didn't need all the bees to go to sleep to keep the wrongness in my mother from getting wronger. We just needed to waste all our wishes.

"Let's go closer," I said.

And then I did the wrong thing.

My Life,
for Promotional Use Only

The building where I work used to be a bank. Now it's lots of little start-ups, private suites, outlaw architects, renegade CPA's, club kids with three-picture deals. It's very artsy in the elevators. Everybody's shaved and pierced in dainty places. They are lords of tiny telephones, keepers of dogs on battery-operated ropes.

I work here for my ex-girlfriend, some sort of handy-man, or some kind of clerk. I can't run an accounting program, or collate, or even reload a stapler right, but there's usually something for me to do, even if it's only to loiter, to stand around in a way that reminds Rosalie she's my boss.

This is not hard.

Rosalie is some kind of rock star now. She's the founder of a web site for serotonin-depleted teenage girls. They log on and rant about their home life to other oppressed teens as far away as Laos, or at least Larchmont. Rosalie's paper-rich since a big tech outfit bought the company. There's a line of clothing, a perfume, maybe a sitcom in the works.

Rosalie and I are still chummy. Maybe she feels sorry for me. Maybe she also resents the way I ditched her back when I was a rock star in actual minor fact. She pays me piss wages and sometimes buys me lunch.

"Let's recap," she'll say, the two of us out for Indian. The condition is I tell her all about my latest girlfriend.

"Her name is Glenda," I say. "She's a painter."

"Painting's very in right now," says Rosalie. "Or it was

a few months ago. I don't have time to keep up."

After me, Rosalie fell in love with a boy billionaire who saw her picture in a fashion spread, one of those bulimia gazettes dedicated to time and the body's dwindle. They had what amounted to an amorous montage, young industrialist and glamorous new media mogulette—Zürich, Paris, Crete. Then one night the kid had a coke seizure, drove his Jeep off a bridge into a lake. For me, there are only two words that count in this story: Electric windows. My father always warned me about them.

"You're in the drink," he said, "and the power shorts out. A dumb way to go."

Maybe they make them differently now. I don't drive much. Maybe the kid hit his head.

These days Rosalie wrestles her Saint Bernard through doors, calls her lawyer from the curb. Whenever she pinches a napkin in half for the big dog's leavings, bends over for a civic-minded scoop, her jeans make this lovely spout of denim at the back. You can see a piece of the prayer wheel she has tattooed on her tailbone. Look hard and maybe you can see me there, too, shackled to the spokes, spinning, dying.

"With Glenda, is it as good as it was with us?" Rosalie says at one of our tandoori lunches. Her mouth is a cavern of cumin.

"It's different," I say.

"Good answer. We just did an issue on why the best ex-boyfriends lie."

"I know," I say, "I was there when you thought it up."

There really is a Glenda the Painter, but she must be in her nineties by now, if she's not dead. She was old when my mother took me to her studio on Saturdays to learn how to draw. I could never get past foreshortening feet, which I took, correctly, I think, to be symptomatic of a deep character flaw. I was some side-on maestro, though. I'd have been hot shit in ancient Egypt.

The first time someone at the office asked me about my skill-set, I thought it was some kind of mail-order frying pan. Everyone seems to have one but me. The people I work with are human résumés. They are fluent in every computer language, boast degrees in marketing and medieval song. They snowboard on everything but snow. They study esoteric forms of South American combat and go on all-deer diets. Sometimes I'm not even sure what they are up to, but I know I will read about it in one of our city's vibrant lifestyle journals. It's easy to detest these people, but they have such energy, such will.

I used to think I had integrity but I came to realize it was just sloth. For a few years I was the lead singer in a band of punk manqués. I couldn't sing, but who could? Talent was not the point. The hard dick of knowingness was pushing the least of us into the light. I referred to myself as the frontman. I liked the word. I was never at the front of anything before.

Our music was in dire need of notes but we had the charm of the improperly medicated. Between songs I used to stab out cigarettes on my tongue, weep, proclaim my love for my father in all its sordid, socially-determined complexity. Everyone said they couldn't make out the words once the music started, but I preferred it that way. God knows what people will think if they ever really hear you.

I met Rosalie when she came to our show at a converted storefront grocery at the edge of the city. Everything was a converted something down there. Every club was the Bakery, the Barber Shop, Shoe Repair. My band was already up on stage, coaxing screeches from defective Peaveys, giving in to the joy of a random cymbal splash. This was our much-theorized intro. My entrance wasn't due for a while, not until all possible frequencies of aural inanity had cancelled themselves out. Soon enough I would crawl into the lights with a microphone in my ass, bleat what I took to be holy.

Now I stepped out to the street in my fur stole and crash helmet, drank off my malt forty. That's when I saw her, Rosalie, standing there in radiant slut-majesty beneath a urine-stained awning. She was talking to a tiny lady who might, in a period of categorical leniency, have passed for dwarf. This lady was selling syringes from a paper bag. I was waiting for her to recognize me, an occasional customer. Rosalie crouched in her pumps, as though smalling herself for some kind of progressive-minded field work with the dwarf. Or maybe she had finally found somebody who, as she tended to put it, really, *really* made sense. I smashed my bottle on a nearby sculpture, this hideous tinwork someone had dragged to the curb, maybe the second-to-last act of its agonized maker.

"The show's started, bitch," I said.

Rosalie wheeled.

I figured she was looking for someone to talk to her that way.

It was a good guess.

We bought an old Merc with turquoise-tipped window handles, drove past green fields and shimmering phallocracies of silo to see her bi-polar brother in Pittsburgh, PA. Going over a river I had a shudder, a sense of the terrible that would not be mine. We checked into a Super 8 motel with a bottle of Maker's Mark bourbon and a running conversation about trust. I said for her to say a secret. She confessed she had never undertaken a proper bowel movement, that only on the rarest of days, fecal baubles, marble-sized things, pressed and shiny, worried themselves through her.

This is something between us now, and I can't say it doesn't affect me on the job. I suffer from lackey bitterness. Treachery is an easy sideways step.

"You should see the woman try to take a dump," I'll tell the design team, looking to comfort them after some venomous memo from Rosalie detailing their failure to achieve a "totalizing space for commerce and dialog."

And here's the other thing: I can't remember the secret I told Rosalie. I must have told her something.

That's how that works, right?

So, what's the story?

What the hell is wrong with me?

Where the hell is my inner soul?

When it looked like our band was going to be the next great revolution in popular idiocy, I broke it off with Rosalie. A teenage industry groomsman took us out for transexually-served gnocchi and told us our time had come. The only thing we needed to do now was concoct some version of music. With all the speedballs and blowjobs coming my way, I figured there'd be little of me left over for some version of Rosalie.

Our double-album debut, *Barbecue Pork Class Suicide*, was snubbed by the mainstream and reviled by the underground. Or maybe it was the reverse. Either way, I can tell you it hurt. When the spiteful alcoholics you have always depended on for uplift turn their backs, it's time to call it a nice post-college try.

Once in a while, though, in the elevator at work, someone will stop me, a man my age with a cell phone, a portfolio case. He will ask me if I am who I am, recall with wonder something I did on stage with safety razors, mayonnaise. Maybe it's some dim gift I've given him, some phony idea that he's reached into danger long enough for one life. Now he can make some calls, do some deals. But neither of us knows what danger is. Neither of us is sinking fast through lake weeds.

Tonight, Rosalie wants to have a drink after work. She sent me e-mail about it from a few desks away. She says she has an errand to run, that she will meet me at this new bar I keep walking past but avoiding, one of those places where they pay slinky women with nose gold to sip peanut-butter martinis and approximate feeling. The errand must be a ruse. Probably Rosalie doesn't want the staff to see us leave together, which, after all the rumor I've spewed, is fine by me.

We sit in bean bags in a low bright room. This is one of those theme bars. Maybe the theme is childhood in suburbia. It doesn't matter, the theme is always the same. The theme is we're not black, after all. Everything is a variation on this theme.

Rosalie calls over the waitress and they talk for a while about somebody's new art gallery. The waitress is famous for a piece where she served Bloody Marys mixed with her menstrual blood. Word had it she overdid the tabasco.

I wait for the moment when our waitress stops being a notorious trangressor of social mores and becomes our waitress again, look for it in her eyes, that sad blink, and order a beer.

"So," says Rosalie, poking through a bowl of Swedish fish, "how are you?"

"Man, those shelves are really coming along. It's a very exciting time."

"You're funny. But forget work. I don't want to talk about work. That's all I do now. Meetings. Meetings. Value triangles."

"The pressure, the pressure."

"No, really. I mean, it's great, but what the hell happened?

Who is this woman talking to you right now? Do you know this woman? Does she bear any resemblance to the little twit who used to follow you around, hang on your every word?"

"I miss that little twit."

"I don't," says Rosalie. "And fuck you, you miss her. I don't miss her at all."

"What?"

"What what? Did you think I was going to spend my whole life trailing you around, soaking up your bullshit? Worshipping you? That was a dark time for me. I learned a lot though, I can say that."

"And your pussy ran like a river," I say.

"True," says Rosalie. "How's Glenda?" She sticks her tits out when she says this. This is what I've always loved about Rosalie. She makes the obvious subtle somehow. This is her art. Or maybe I've just always been smitten by her tits.

"Glenda's in bad shape," I say.

"Oh my God, what happened?"

"I don't want to talk about it," I say.

"I know, I know. I can't talk about Kyle and it's a year later."

"So," I say, "are we going to have a commiseration fuck, or what? I have shelves to build."

I have no subtlety when it comes to Rosalie. It's what I've always counted on her loving about me.

We do that thing of lying in bed and touching each other softly like we're brother and sister on a naughty expedition. We do that thing of falling asleep feeling all sad and superior to fools who fuck. I've never been too keen on this particular activity, but it's good to do once in a while, keeps you sharp for the day you may rejoin the human species. It's a nice dense lull in the thin-seeming quick. The only thing is, Rosalie falls asleep before I do, and now I'm up on an elbow studying one of her tits, the way it slinks off and gathers at her top rib, the skin smoothed out on her chest bone. I pull on myself, wonder how I can get my teeth on her nip without violating this cuddle paradigm we've got going, and also without enacting that babyman suckle which would probably sicken us both, not to mention Shrike, the dog, who's heaped near us, brooding on his usurpation. Rosalie turns over and I see those prayer-wheel spokes sticking out past her panties. The swirls have begun to fade.

Next thing there's light in the room and Rosalie's sitting up. I guess she dresses, but somehow I miss it. The dog is doing his big dumb click dance on the hardwood.

"See you at work," she says.

"Wait," I say, "did this happen or not happen?"

"Nothing happened," she says. "So I don't care if it happened or not."

"We can talk about it later," I say.

"Or not," says Rosalie.

I suddenly have the feeling of wanting to confess all my sins, all that back-daggering, those terrible things I say when she steps out of the office for a coffee or a smoke. I want to tell her something she doesn't know about me.

"Glenda's dead," I say.

"Who?" says Rosalie, and leaves.

I pop a Paxil from Rosalie's medicine chest and go downstairs for some Cuban coffee.

I used to come here in the mornings when Rosalie and I were serious, work on my hangover, cool my head on all this anti-Castro Formica, wait for sentience to return like a mildly sadistic soccer coach. Then I'd call the band, hammer out the day's futile itinerary, not much—a few hours of noise in our practice room, then off to the German's where the Butcher of Ludlow Street poured stiff ones, or off to someone's couch for the short-count foil packets and the same dumb saga about some band from Akron, or Toledo, that flamed out years ago but made one choice single somebody's cousin owned. It's a good life if you don't die, or worse, start to believe in it.

The old Cuban and the young Cuban are still there behind the glass case with their pork and pickle sandwiches, still giving me that look. I've never quite known the meaning of it. There have been times, I must admit, it seemed almost accusatory, as though I were on some kind of jack-ass authenticity hunt. Mostly I took it as tender beseechment, a beckon porkward. Either way I've never given them anything to base a look on. I've never even said "Thank you."

"Thank you," I say, today.

"You're welcome," says the young Cuban.

"Thank you," I say again.

If I believed in brief moments of cosmic alignment, I would have to say things feel fairly aligned right now. Better than aligned. I'm one up on universal niceties.

Then I realize I'm still in love with Rosalie, or Rosalie's tit, or Rosalie's tattoo. This must be why they call them brief moments.

I sit there until I'm good and tardy.

It's almost lunch by the time I get to work. This used to be somewhat allowable, but Rosalie has made an effort of late to make us quiet and punctual and professional-seeming in our one big room, all on account of the corporate types who have been dropping by to inspect their acquisition. I'm sure they want us to stay "funky," but it's not as though we turn a profit, and our salaries and overhead are siphoned from their graver silicon concerns. Our parent company makes simulations of hypothetical amphibious invasions for the Navy, and also some kind of spree-killer game for the kids. Rosalie gets pretty jumpy when the men in tasseled loafers pop by.

This one, though, he's got on suede sneakers with his suit. The new breed. He's a smarm engine, torquing himself over Rosalie's work module. He talks in a hush and Rosalie offers up her specialty, low moans and conversational coos floating up from the seat of her lust like observation balloons. Everyone else is locked into monitor glow, code jockeys with their Linux books open on their laps, producers scanning the latest posts from Cyberbitch5.

"I've always been partial to low-hanging fruit," I hear the company man say.

Rosalie waves me over.

"This is Gene," Rosalie tells me. "Gene knew Kyle."

"And I know you!" says Gene.

"I don't think so," I say.

"I doubt you remember, except that we once French kissed. Think back, Chicago, ninety-two, ninety-three. You guys opened for somebody. I can't remember. I can't remember because you were so fucking awesome. You blew my mind. I mean blew it open. I was up front, just a little high school shit. I'd never seen anything like it. Oh my God, Rosalie, you should have seen it."

"Oh, I've seen it," says Rosalie.

"And this guy, he goes down to all the men in the room and starts trying to kiss them. I mean kiss them with these real gentle kisses. Unbelievable. I mean, it was Chicago, okay?

Shaking it all up, this guy. I was so turbo'd. A whole new thing. A whole new idea. No rock bullshit. You know? I mean, sure, it had been done before. I mean, maybe you guys were pretty derivative. But still. Like little butterfly kisses. And the music, man, if it even was music, if it even needed to fall under the rubric of music. Shaking it up. Changing the terms. The terms of the experience. Not just sexually, either. Not just with the microphone in your ass. And what was that stuff you said about the corporate police state? You know, that we had a choice, that we had to choose between a police state or a police state? That really stuck with me. I admired it, man. Truly. All of it. Really. It altered me. Somehow. I don't know how, but I wouldn't be me if I hadn't seen it. You know? Look, I'm scaring him. He's like, Back off, man. Hey, it's cool. But I've got to tell you, I was so psyched when Rosalie told me you were on our team. It all fell together for me when I heard. Rosalie was like, You probably never heard of him, but I hired this guy…Never heard of him! Shit. It all fell together. Here's a guy, I've seen musical equipment in his ass, I've seen him literally crying and shitting and bleeding because the rest of us were too scared to, and here's me, right, always thinking to myself, I saw that, that moved me, so how come I wind up here, doing this? You know, like am I a sell-out? Because I wondered about that. But now you're here. You're here where I am and we're doing this thing together. So, now I'm like, oh, right, this is what we should be doing. You know? The next step. It all falls together now."

"It really, *really* makes sense," says Rosalie.

"Total," says Gene.

"So what's the deal with you?" says Gene. "Are you still playing music?"

"No," I say.

"No? Well, I'm going to sign you up for the company talent show. We do it every year at this great club. It's for real, I mean it's not bullshit. There's a programmer at our San Francisco office who does poetry slams."

"You've got to be fucking kidding," I say.

"No," says Gene. "It's going to be awesome."

There's another e-mail from Rosalie asking me to meet her later in the stairwell. It's our unofficial conference room, though there are plans for expanding into the suite next door. I diddle around on the web for a while, do my umpteenth search on the name of my old band. It's pathetic, I guess, but it beats the heartbreak of a scrapbook. It's always the same hits, too. Some kid in Bremen selling bootlegs, a girl in Wisconsin who posted a review of our last ever show. "They sucked," she wrote, "and in sucking proved their point about American consumerism. We won't see the likes of this band again." I used to have a fantasy about flying out to Green Bay to sweep her off her feet, but I tended to sabotage the dream by playing out the scenario to the finish. Little girl grows up and sees through me, puts an end to her dark time.

I hear Shrike's barks long before I see Rosalie. She's down on one knee with the big boy in a tender headlock. He's got a wet biscuit in his mouth, jerks his snout around, lays into me with a sloppy eyeball as though he knows something I don't.

"Did you hear that," I say, "Gene worships me. I forever altered his consciousness. Think I have a shot at V.P.?"

"We need to talk," says Rosalie.

"Last night," I say.

"That, too," says Rosalie.

We talk there in the stairwell. Much is noted about my

underutilization in the company structure, even more about my eclectic skill-set going to menial waste. Rosalie doesn't really fire me. I don't really quit. Somehow, though, it seems I'm out of a job.

"Does Gene know about this?" I say. I picture him hearing of my departure, looking up from the Full Amphibious Scenarios: Weehauken demo running on his desktop, stunned, worried about the talent show.

"Gene supports the idea," says Rosalie. "But it's up to you."

"What about us?" I say.

"I think we need to move on in all aspects of our lives. You're not happy here."

"How do you know?"

"If you were happy, you wouldn't be so busy denouncing my style of bowel evacuation to the staff."

"I'm sorry," I say, and probably mean it.

"It's okay," says Rosalie.

"Fine," I say. "But I want you to know I love you."

"I love you, too," she says. Fraught. Considered. Her delivery makes my declaration sound cheap.

"I'll clear out my things," I say.

"No rush," says Rosalie, and starts to push the dog down the stairs.

"Wait," I say.

"What?"

"Let me ask you something. In the motel. When we went to see your brother."

"Yeah?"

"What was my secret?"

"Are you testing me?"

"No."

"That's sad. You don't remember? That's really sad."

"I know. I can't remember my secret. What the hell was my secret? I must have had something I was running from. What the hell is wrong with me?"

"Nothing's wrong with you," says Rosalie. "You peaked a little early. It happens sometimes."

"Rosalie, tell me my goddamn secret," I say.

"I've got to go."

"The show's over, bitch," I call, but too softly, as though my throat knows to close it off.

I clear out quietly. I don't really have any things.

I go over to the bean-bag bar. The door is locked and I look through the window. There are no bean bags there. There are some stacked boxes and a broom. Maybe it's a new theme.

Somewhere in this city somebody is probably peaking right now, getting high on a couch and talking about a bootleg he bought from a kid in Bremen. I should locate this fool, tell him what a lout he is, but he's all I've got.

Too bad I sold the Merc. I could sail it off the Verrazano. I'd be a footnote to a footnote, food for carp.

Maybe I'll fly out to Wisconsin, instead. Or take some slow hearse of a bus. They have movies on the good lines now, so you don't get so bitter about the landscape, big windows that open with manual levers in case of bad aquatic luck.

Torquemada

The crazy thing is I'm not even Jewish. But when I showed up at Dana's house with that beanie on my head, her dad didn't even blink an eye. Maybe that's because he doesn't have any. Well, he does, but I think he pops them out at night before he goes to bed. Dunks them in a water glass. Actually, I'm not sure if that's true. I know he can't see. At least he can't see me.

Dana got mad and told me to take the beanie off. She called it the harmonica. "Take it off, you idiot," she said.

"Take what off," I said.

"That fucking harmonica," she said.

"Why," I said, "Is this Spain?"

Dana didn't know what I was talking about because she's not in World Studies. She's in all these college-track classes. But they don't teach her shit.

Dana gets mad at me all the time.

Like when I try to squeeze her sno-balls behind the maintenance shed fifth period.

"Get your fucking hands off me," she says. "We're in school, you idiot. You'll get us expelled."

"Nobody ever gets expelled," I tell her.

It's true.

Except for the time Steve Redillia stuck a knife in John Preston's ear. Other than that, no one gets kicked out. And no one in the history of Nearmont Regional High School East ever got the boot for copping an honest feel—off his own girlfriend no less.

Hey, we live on a chunk of dirt called America.

We have a little piece of paper.

It's called the fucking Constitution.

But Dana is a terminal Jervis, and she's always getting pretty pissed. Like if I spark a bone in her car, or make her blow off a stop-sign, or make her pull over so I can tag that sign (because I'm a tagger, and a legend in this town), or all three in whatever order, Dana gets pissed.

"You're going to get us busted," she says.

"Nobody ever gets busted," I tell her.

Which is not truly true. Chief Howie arrests me all the time. He's some kind of uncle of mine, from the alcoholic semi-retarded branch of the family (like there are others) and he arrests me whenever he feels like it. For whatever. Sometimes just to talk.

Like tonight when I'm tagging the dumpster behind Dave's Good Spirits Wine and Liquor all bent out because of Dana and the beanie incident, with her thinking I was goofing on her religion when I'd just been thinking about the whole Torquemada thing because of this report I gave for Ms. Fredericks's class and felt bad for Dana because they would have fucked with her in Spain and just wanting to show my solidarity and finding in my closet this beanie from when my neighbor Todd Feld had that party at the Jewish temple and they gave out free beanies at the door with his name on it so I'm standing in her living room with the Todd Feld Autograph Beanie on my head and Dana's being a total cunt and then I hear her dad shuffling around at the top of the stairs going "Dana, Dana," like he's going to ask her where he put his eyes because they're not in the glass and since weirdness always increases exponentially I throw the beanie down on the rug and bolt, saying "I'll be back," but of course it comes out more squirmdog than superheroic, and now I'm here alone behind Dave's when Chief Howie pulls up in his cruiser.

"Got a minute?" says Chief Howie.

"Busy," I say. I roll the almost empty spray can under the dumpster with my foot and lean up against the tag, hoping the paint's as quick-dry as advertised.

"Wrong answer," says Chief Howie, and gets out of the car. He comes over like a TV cracker sheriff and administers the beat-down, cuffs me and throws me in the back seat, careful to press my head going in like they do on all the shows. We drive up Spartakill Road, past the Burger King and the Hobby Shop and the Pitch-n-Putt, until we're going by all the big houses with the huge lawns I used to mow and the big bay windows that you can look through if you want to see people alone or in groups feeling like shit and not knowing why.

"People up here treat me like the garbage man. Which is what I am." Chief Howie winks in the rearview. "Know what that makes you?" He takes a pull from something in his hand. I can hear bottles clinking together on the rubber floormat.

"Don't worry about me," I say.

"Why would I worry about you?" says Chief Howie.

We turn on Venus, cop wheels crunching on the gravel edge of someone's driveway. I make out the shapes in the darkness, gigantic mounds of earth, big sleeping tractors, rows of brand-new houses wrapped in moonglow plastic. I've been up this way already tonight because at the end of the drive is the model house where Dana and her father and her father's eyeballs live. It's Dana's cousin's company's development, but so far they're the only customers.

"That dumb hebe," says Chief Howie.

I don't say anything because I don't know what he knows about me and Dana, if he's actually trying to fuck with me or we're just up here because he felt like driving, because if you are just driving around it makes some sense to end up here if you're curious about what all the dark shapes are and then one with a few lights on in it.

The lights are out in Dana's living room and you can see the TV screen reflected in the big front window. It's hard to tell exactly what's on the screen, but what it looks like it is is pussies. That's right—in the plural, shaved and flaming, smooching in a close-up grind. What's a blind man doing with porn? Or is it Dana? Stretched out on the couch, spelunking with one hand and pinching her little sno-balls with the other.

I see Chief Howie has taken a sudden interest in the cinema. I see he's staring at the window, too.

"My, my," he says. "There ought to be a law about that."

"There is, Sheriff," I say. "It's called the fourth amendment. Privacy and shit."

"You little fuck!" says Chief Howie, whips a bottle back over the seat at my head. The ability to duck is a perfect example of why the nature-versus-nurture argument Dana's always yapping about is a pile of crap. It's both. Still, what does it get you? There you are, cuffed in the back seat while your pissed-off retard cop-uncle pulls off the curb and drives you far, far away from the big soft couch where your girlfriend is all alone with her juicer on frappé, just hoping you'll come back like you half-assed threatened to, and now you are driving cruel distances from anything that could be reasonably called joy. So the bottle doesn't open a big red smile on your forehead. So fucking what?

There's no question left in my mind that this Saturday night is shot, is history, is a tiny meaningless point on the time lines Ms. Fredericks makes us copy down in World Studies. Chief Howie dumps me down at the bottom of the hill, takes off the cuffs, "impounds" my shake, my papers, a few bucks from my wallet.

"Go home," says Chief Howie, and peels off like somewhere there's a crime being perpetrated besides his own sorry-assed life.

A brisk nipplebreeze jaunt across the moonlit links of the Nearmont Country Club and I find myself once more in a familiar spot, leaning on the big white birch in front of Steve Redillia's house, wondering whether I really want to go in there again.

As part of my project to ascertain whether I really want to go in there again, I crouch down in the bushes next to Steve Redillia's house and peek through the basement window. Bilious smoke of the kind hangs nimbus-like in the half-lit room, and there's Steve Redillia flopped out on his ratty couch, headphones on, Zildjian sticks flying in tight four/four air-drum formation. Steve Redillia is the third best speed metal drummer in New Jersey, or so he was told by Archbishop Chickenhawk of the Non-Dead, when he tried out for them and didn't get the gig, and so he has repeatedly informed us.

I hate listening to music with him, not only because so-called speed metal is slow as shit as far as I'm concerned, but because he's the type who when you listen to a song with him will in the middle of it nod his head and say, "Nice," like in the middle of all that double-kick-drumming and guitar he heard some subtle shit your dolt ass could never comprehend. Then, if you don't immediately smile and agree with him, Steve Redillia gives you this look, goes off on how nobody actually *listens* to music, and then maybe starts throwing shit, with you, as closest representative of a species he detests, the target.

"You fucking twats don't get it at all!" he'll say. "Goddamn puppets on a string!" And then objects, sharp and heavy, will receive the gift of flight.

Fuck it.

I book.

I'm coming home to a beat-down either way, so why procrastinate? I'm standing outside the kitchen door looking in, and now it's like the third time tonight I'm sneaking around windows like a perv. Dad's on the phone, probably with the Big Chief himself. Dad's leaning up on the refrigerator—and I swear to God I catch him pulling one of those stringy boogers out of his nose, the kind with the dry handle and the gooey tail. He pulls it all the way out, holds it up for inspection, and then, I swear on Dana's dad's missing eyes, my fucking progenitor reaches under the edge of the Formica and deposits the snot jewel.

When I was a crawling babyboy, I used to hang out under that Formica, tagging the cabinets with my orange crayon, and whenever I looked up, I always saw these dried snots like tiny cave spikes dangling down. Once Mom found them there and chewed my ass but I denied it, which just got her madder, and Dad was sitting there the whole time shaking his head even though we both knew they were his boogers. I remember a look on his face like it's a shame the world is like this before he got up with his belt.

Not to say this event was some big revelation, like before this he was taking me to the hobby shop on Saturdays and teaching me how to fly kites and shit, and then suddenly everything changed. It's just another point on the time line.

So I go around to the garage door, hoping to get in that

way—but Dad must have cloned himself, or built replicants, because by the time I get there I see another one of him through the garage window standing under the lightbulb with the only sound the hum of the meat freezer. He's surrounded by all his tools, his hands on his hips like he's the royal torturer taking a moment to reflect on the hot debate of the day, the rack versus the thumbscrews.

I guess this occurs to me because for Ms. Fredericks's class I made that report on the Spain Inquisition situation. "A bit over the top, but informative," was how Ms. Fredericks described my report, because I went into detail about the various devices any good torturer was familiar with, like the special skillets to fry up your testicles and the two-handed saws they wedged up your ass to saw you in half with.

Some of the Jervises in my class were all offended or something, like I approved of the whole thing (though no doubt Steve Redillia, if he hadn't been expelled, would have), like I wasn't fucking going out with a Jewish girl anyway, wasn't sensitive to what her feelings might be in regards to Torquemada, if anybody were to tell her what the man thought of her, instead of seeing that I was just trying to do what any decent historian would try to do, too, namely to describe all the sick shit that went down, which Ms. Fredericks says must be done so we learn from our mistakes and so history doesn't keep happening again and again. But I have my doubts about that theory. Because like remembering or not remembering your last beat-down has shit to do with the next one coming at your ass. And what help is a skinny black line with dots on it besides just to say this sucked, and that sucked, and do not doubt it all will suck again?

Less Tar

Out on the street I'm thinking, "Who needs life, people?" I stop off at Gupta's to buy cigarettes. I've quit quitting them again.

"Two?" says Gupta, goes to the carton on the shelf, my carton, the soft-packs, lays them on the countertop. Forty sticks of friendship there.

"How's your brother?" I say.

"Doing the same as you," he says, pinches thumb and finger to his lips. Gupta was a journalist somewhere where it's okay to torture one for prying. Lucky he had a brother set up in America. Now he sells Salems and bongs and screw-top one-hitters to the kids cutting trig at the prep school down the block.

"Your brother and I," I say, "we must have a death wish."

"Don't be a fool," says Gupta, "no one really wishes it."

First smoke in a week. My lungs are good and rested, strong and wet. One drag, another, and the great dense mist of things—the company, Katrine—drifts up, away. When the butt burns down to my fingers I'll flick it into the street, light another for the short walk home. I'll put on some records, re-read my junk mail, scour the clause minutia in the sweepstakes offers, call Katrine's machine. I'll smoke and I'll smoke and I'll smoke.

Smoking at work, that's another story. We are outlaws of the state. We have a hideout, a floor forsaken partway through remodeling. Ghost cubes, glass-walled tombs. We all found our way here somehow. Martha runs the newsstand in the lobby. Mikhail is the Russian super's lackey, possibly his son. Rich teaches real estate a few floors up. I do ad sales for an on-line magazine. I let them think I'm some kind of player, a silicon prince on the make, but Rich knows enough to see the fear in my eyes. I've been tracking numbers of doom these days.

"Don't worry," he tells me, "maybe you'll fail upwards."

Comments like this are why I'm always encouraging Rich to quit smoking. Who needs a smart-ass during your moments of stress-reduction?

Here's Mikhail in a busted chair, some ergonomic locus of swivel and command. He flicks ash into a plastic cup. It's a corner office, nothing here but dead carpet. I think of Gupta, wonder if it was a room like this where they did what they did to him, whip and wire and bamboo shoot, a rubber bucket for the human run-off of him.

Mikhail is runty in the big chair.

"Yo, I'm the CEO," he says. "Your ass is fired!"

"You're going to have to buy my shares, Mike." I tap a cigarette out of the pack and tug it free with my teeth. Mikhail does silver magic with his Zippo, cups me flame. A team. A family.

"How's the boss treating you?" I say. "Working hard or hardly working?"

Up here, I'm only good for pleasantries, the national patter.

"Work is for bitches," says Mikhail, puts two fingers out, ash tweezed between them. His thumb is hammer-cocked. "A cap to the motherfucking dome. Know what I mean? Fuck toil, bro."

"I'm with you," I say, my words weak, unmeant, me here in French blue, an office-brightener tie. There's grit in the combs of his thermal shirt, dull smears in his pants. His father, the super, sends him crawling through the ducts and tunnels of this heap. Asbestos hunts. The job, he told me, is to tack up false partitions, fool the Haz-Mat guys.

"I should learn computers," says Mikhail, "they use them in the big buildings, niggers like me be using them for air-conditioning and shit."

"Niggers?"

"That's right."

Mikhail gets up on the window sill, chops the air, slips a wire back into the smoke alarm.

"What about me?" I say.

"Guess you done slid the python eyes, G."

We bump fists like ballplayers do.

I'm down.

Every few months I get another newsletter from the National Smokers' Brigade. How do they know? An eye in the sky? An intercepted e-mail? Each time I have to remember the last time I was drunk, the last time I ever even drank. There was a guy at the bar, goatee and a patriotic T-shirt, "Don't Tread on Me," that colonial snake. He had a clipboard with a pen on a string. He rambled on about Jefferson, Rousseau, jabbed that pen around. I guess I must have signed the form. This was years ago. I don't remember much. The night ended the next morning in the emergency room, a doctor with another clipboard, a metal one, hinged.

"Why do you do it, son?" the doctor asked.

"Go shoot a speedball," I told him, "and you'd never ask anybody that question again."

Some people give up the cigarettes with everything else.

Me, I was pretty sure that without nicotine I'd be swinging from the shower nozzle in no time. You have to keep something between yourself and the truth of yourself or you're dead, was how I figured it. Still do.

The upshot is that I get this newsletter from time to time, bumper stickers, membership pins. The Brigade, I gather, is funded by the tobacco lobby, but they play themselves up grassroots, an astroturf campaign. It's always the same lead story in the newsletter, a trucker bar somewhere that won't comply with the local smoking laws. The goose-steppers, the anti-smoke Gestapo, they've shut the joint down. We threw all of our boys and Patton at them, but the Reich has finally won. Or maybe it's the Reds. Either way the barmaid can't make rent and the Constitution is a paper scrap borne off on criminal winds. No veterinary school for the barmaid's son. He's headed for the mills.

Those anti-smoking bastards, I'll think, spark up another square. Then I remember there is no barmaid, no son, and I start to hack up sour chunks of myself, toss my cigarette in the can. Still, it would be nice to stay pissed, to get my hands on a Ruger, or a Desert Eagle, join the brigade. We would puff away in a toolshed and plot the nicotine secession. Let us not forget, one of us would rasp, there are millions like us, ready to die for freedom.

Dying for something, anything, is tricky, though. You'd better be sure you believe. There was a time, I must admit, I might have been willing to die for Katrine. Or at least, as she would say, *discuss the possibility*. We had a good amount of discussion before we called it quits. Breaking up, she said, should take at least as long as the together part. Otherwise, what was the point? Even when we knew it was over, each of us was waiting for the other to make the move, to assume the mantle of villainy, to blink. She *blinked*, I told myself when she finally left, like maybe here I was—Jack the Man. I was watching a lot of the History Channel then. I pictured footage of me in deep conference with my close advisors. What if there's a CIA inside the CIA? What if she screwed that guy at work?

The greeting on Katrine's answering machine, it's so honeyed, so wise. Anyone would marry that voice, those cadences, those warm conjunctive halts. Sometimes I call just to hear her sing her poem, the one fashioned of a certain disappearance—"I'm not here right now"—and her deep sweet oath to "get back real soon." Like the solution to a riddle that will spring the maiden from the dragon's lair, all you have to do is speak the digits, say your telephone number into the machine, but even that's too much for me. I let the tape roll out. I am the insufficient son, the older, gruffer one that fails at the cave mouth, back broken on the stones, guts strung up in trees. My type has a seemly sibling who will prevail.

I hang up, draw another smoke from the foil.

All it takes is a morning with the spreadsheets to glimpse the four horsemen of fiscal apocalypse thundering toward our dream of an IPO. There's Plummeting Ad Sales, in his scorched robes, on his maggot-shot horse, waving a scythe. I bolt from my desk, pass two design guys in the next room arguing about the new homepage art. Don't bother, I want to tell them, but in this business you can trash a perfectly good career leaking catastrophe an hour before it's official.

Martha is in the corner office, cooing smoke. It's hard to tell Martha's age, but the drop of her face, the veins in her hands, remind me of my mother right before she got sick.

When your mother is dead, maybe every woman over a certain age reminds you of her. You'll find it in an eyebrow, the varicose nova on a stubbly calf, beckoning you to bury your head on her breast and weep.

My advice: Don't do it.

"How are you, Martha?"

"Fucking pricks don't pay for their newspapers," she says. "Grab one, say 'Get you next time, honey!' Get fucking this next time! I got rent, you know."

"Tell me about it."

"I am, you moron."

"I know that, Martha," I say.

"Fuck you, too," she says, flips her More to the carpet, grinds it out with her espadrille. "You pricks are all the same."

True, and probably I owe Martha a few bucks myself, but the way things are going I'll need them. Now Rich walks in, a silver pin stuck in his lapel, his hair slicked back in the style of men who seem to be saying, Hey, go blow, my hair is slicked back, and on weekends I know joy.

"Big doings on your floor, buddy. I'm smelling napalm."

"What?"

"My only advice for you is to remember to tape the bottom of the box. Got a light?"

It hits me in the stairwell, that pin. The Smoker's Brigade. Comrade. We could start a cell here in the building, rig Martha with dynamite girdles, send Mikhail on recon jobs through ventilation ducts into the Lysol'd HQ's of pink-lungers. Rich and I would vie for the fealty of our troops until one of us, probably me, came up python eyes in his biopsy. Unwilling to wheeze my way to the Great Smoking Section Beyond, I'd pass my Desert Eagle over to Rich and shut my eyes.

"Savor the fine tobacco flavor for me, Sport," he'd say, thumb the hammer back.

"Fuck toil, bro!" Mikhail would shout.

"Do the prick," Martha would hiss.

Downstairs, everyone is weeping and hugging, or readying a lawsuit. There's a rented cop in my cube.

"Personal files only," he says.

The boss sticks his head in, his face flushed, teary, trauma-elated.

"You were great," he says. "You did great work. We all did. They didn't give me a chance. I could have turned this thing around."

"I missed your speech," I say.

"Anything I can do for you, let me know," he says. I almost ask him to hold down the tape at the bottom of the box.

When my mother was dying I kept going down to the street to smoke. You would think I would be some kind of pariah lighting up outside a cancer ward, but no one paid any mind. Bald men, bald women, bald teens sat out in the summer twilight in their gowns. Cut open, sewn shut, garlanded with IV lines, poisoned with their futile glowing cures, they puffed away like wild heroes.

I would stand nearby and remember a day when I was not much more than six, seven, see myself sitting on a beach with my mother and father, the two of them slung low in canvas chairs beneath a striped umbrella, smoking, drinking sodas, laughing over secret words, sticking their filter-tips into the sand.

That day I stood up before them with all the theater of the

firstborn child, my feet clamped to the cement lip of the artificial lake our town had built for us, our neighbors, whomever else was good and kind and willing to pay. It was early summer and my birthday was, as my mother had noted, on the horizon. I pictured it a pack mule in the distance, heaped with trinkets, absolution, cheer.

"What do you want for your big day?" my father asked.

He wore the sideburns of his time, the kind no retro-styling can ever seem to honor. We are Saigon, those sideburns said, Altamont, Nixon under the rotary gust. We are heart-smashed and uncertain and looking to score. My father, with those whiskers, was one of reason's priests, on the lam from chaos, cabal, a lit stick of disaffection in his lips.

My mother, she was spilling out of her swimming suit cups in all her freckled wonder, moving maybe past voluptuous motherhood into some other great, rippling power. The coils of her hair were lit up with warning flares of white. She visored her eyes with her hand, regarded me as she often did, as though secretly awaiting the moment I would cease to astonish her with my devotion.

"Yes, honey, what do you want? Another Tonka toy?"

That birthday animal lumbered up, buckled under lashed-down treasures—injection-molded soldiers, many-speeded bikes. Beyond the beast stood me, a vision of me, the most perfect boy the world has ever known.

"What I want for my birthday," I said, "all I want, is for both of you to stop smoking."

It was my moment of genius, if it is true we are each of us blessed with one. They quit, of course, for a while, at least. Wouldn't you, if you were as strong and beautiful as my mother and my father were one summer when our town built a beach?

I stop off at Gupta's. He's flipping through a skin mag, all those smears of color, angles of receipt.

"That's what my ex-girlfriend looks like," I say.

"Is this what you did to her," says Gupta, "or what you saved her from?"

"I said looked like her. How's it going?"

"Very well," he says. "I've got an assignment. A magazine overseas. Real money."

"What about this one here?" I say.

"I'm not talented enough to write for this one. I don't know all the ways to describe the big tit."

"You can learn that," I say. "You just have to care."

Gupta laughs, reaches back to my carton, the soft-packs.

"No," I say.

"Box?" There's a shade of panic in his voice, the order of things thrown.

"No," I say.

"What do you want?"

"I forgot," I say.

"No one forgets," says Gupta. "You didn't forget. Our brains carry blueprints for a thousand years. There is no such thing as forgetting. You just can't find it right now."

"So, in a thousand years someone will remember what I wanted just now?" I picture a man like me, a man of my build, my coloring, my gait, stitched, gathered, helix'd with my codes. He sits in his commuter pod and whistles through space, maybe en route to Jupiter to sell some ads. A vision of Katrine, stepping out of the bath tub, explodes with the terror of endless sameness in his mind.

"Exactly," says Gupta, pounds his fist on a great glossy ass.

I'm almost out the door when I remember.

"I know what I want," I say. "I want something new. Something light. Less tar."

Gupta slides the gleaming thing across the counter. There's a new world there inside the package, new words ringed around the paper, new speckles on the tip. Life, people, happiness, a jaunty, easeful kind of breathing. I've seen print ads for this brand, admired them, or more than admired them. I have communed with them. They have spoken to me from billboards, from the backs of scented magazines—no cowboys, no mountaineers, just a handsome couple poised at the end of a plush settee. Maybe they're Katrine and me, hosting a party, the heave of voices, the crush and chatter, friends in the living room, on the threshold, in the vestibule, the two of us puffing there so elegant, our free hands laced together on the cushions, our free hands squeezing, pulsing words of oath: I Love You, I Love You, Let's Make it Work, I Love You So Much, Let's Not Ever Ever Quit.

Sam Lipsyte was born in 1968 and grew up in New Jersey. He has been a noise-rock frontman, a cold-caller, and an editor at *Feed* magazine in New York City, where he lives. This is his first book.

Thanks to everyone for the wise and encouraging words, especially Gordon Lish, Ira Silverberg, Samantha Gillison, J.J. Gifford, Steven Johnson, Stefanie Syman, Amanda Griscom, Alex Abramovich and the good ship *Feed*, Carol Irving, Ted Grossman, Ceridwen Morris, Farhad Sharmini, Jacqueline Humphries, Cynthia Weiner, Carol Greene, Robert Reynolds, Paul Fleming, Mallory Tarses, Will Eno, Michael Kimball, Robert Lipsyte, Susannah Lipsyte, and Ben Nachumi. Thanks to Joanna Yas, Daniel Pinchbeck, and everyone at Open City Books. Thanks to Deborah Barkow.

Thanks to Robert Bingham.

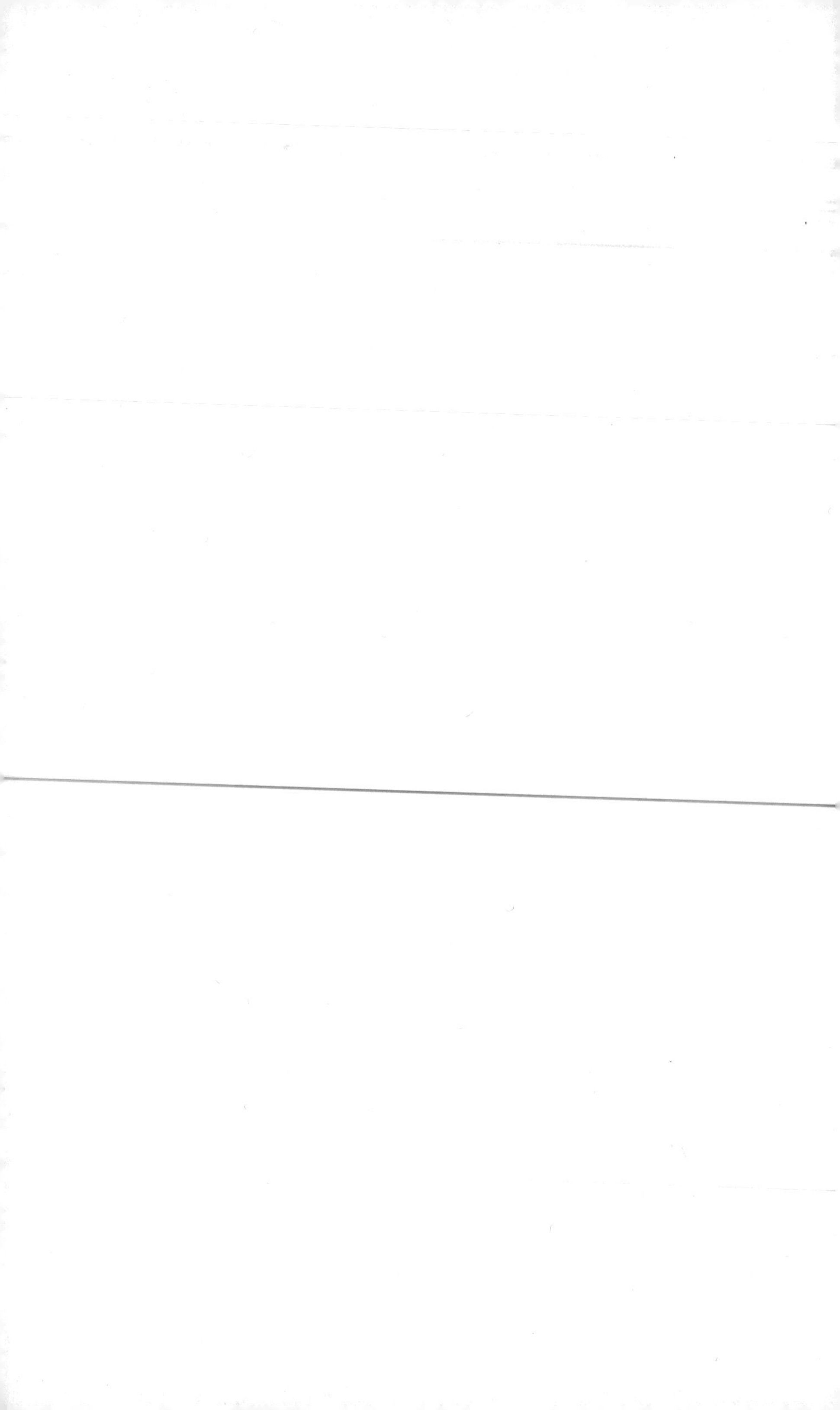